A GLIMPSE OF ARCADIA

MACDONALD HASTINGS

A Glimpse of Arcadia

Coward-McCann, Inc.   New York

Little known part of London's history

To the memory of my friend
MICHAEL JOSEPH

CONTENTS

A GLIMPSE OF ARCADIA

I

THE TIDE OF MARCH

IT was that bleak night of March 21st, 1861, when to the superstitious Big Ben presaged disaster by striking twenty times at three o'clock in the morning. The old man and the boy in a leaky rowboat, who drifted on the ebbing-tide from Greenwich Pier to Bugsby's Hole, were too far downstream to hear it; although if it was indeed a portent, as simple people said, Big Ben might have tolled for them. And for the silver fish that ran that night up London River.

The boy, his head and shoulders pocketed in a hood fashioned out of a hopsack, his bare feet and legs streamered with Thames slime, crouched in his rags over the oar which he held rudderwise in a notch in the stern of the wherry. Underneath him the bilge water slapped about in the gratings. The raw wind, blowing upstream from the estuary, licked the threadbare basket of his ribs and made his nose drip saltwater like a faulty tap.

It would have been difficult to guess his age. His normal growth had been arrested by lack of proper food and his lungs were laden with the soot-blackened air of the warrens of the waterfront. But, emaciated though he was, his peaked face was luminous with vitality. As he watched the shadowy figure of the old man his eyes had the bright wariness of a mouse and his hands, covering half the leather-bound handle of the oar, managed the boat with the cunning of a skilled waterman.

He was thirteen. The old man was his grandfather. How old the old man was the old man didn't rightly know himself. He reckoned that he was seventy; but he must have been considerably more.

'Where we goin', Pa?'

'Dead Man's Island.'

'Ain't much coal in the mud there. Weren't last time.'

'We ain't lookin' for coal.'

'We ain't got any, Pa.'

'I said we ain't lookin' for coal. That's what I said.'

The old man spat into the swirling black water of the river. His own skinny frame was wrapped in an ancient sea-cloak with a hair blanket laid on top of that. On his head he wore a black chimney-pot hat with a burst rim. He was bowed down in the well of the boat, mumbling to himself, hawking tobacco juice, and clawing with vein-knotted talons in the mesh of a seine-net, buoyed with corks and heeled with lead, which was heaped between his legs.

Fold by fold, at the full swing of his arm, he was clearing refuse out of the seine before settling the netting to his satisfaction at his feet. He worked by the light of a lantern, fed with sperm oil, which guttered dimly under the bow-thwart.

Sometimes he looked up to check his bearing as the boy manœuvred the boat round the looming shapes of the craft anchored in the tideway; lumpy paddle steamers, broad-beamed barges, square-rigged sailing ships with stepped masts and lowered yards and, hard by Greenwich, the dis-

masted hulk of a wooden man-of-war, once a first-rate ship
of the line and now a seaman's hospital.

As the old man worked, the boy stretched an arm into
the water to snatch at fragments of timber and once at an
apple floating in a scummy eddy. He took a bite out of it
but the sour juice stung his lips and he flung it back into
the water.

As they slipped through Greenwich Reach the banks of
the river on the townside were dotted with the yellow spots
of fish-tailed gaslights. The craft, riding at anchor, lying
straight downstream in the pull of the tide, glimmered with
mooring lights. But at that hour the Thames, so crowded
and noisy in daytime, slept. The only other vessel that
moved was a police galley patrolling off the Isle of Dogs.

The boy sighted it. Half rising, he worked the oar to
bring the wherry behind the shelter of a barge.

'What's narkin' you?' grumbled the old man.

'Peelers.'

'Them bastards. We ain't got nothing aboard. Or 'ave
we?' He raised his elbow threateningly. 'Whatcher been up
to? Come on, or I'll bash you.'

The boy cowered.

'It's only some baccy. I got it off a barge in Limehouse
Reach.'

'Where is it?'

'In the locker.'

''Ow much?'

''Bout five pounds. I thought it was cocoa till I broached
it.'

The police galley hailed them. With a wriggle the boy
slipped off the wet seat and, kneeling in the gratings, opened
the locker with the intention of jettisoning the stolen stuff

overboard. Leaning forward the old man grabbed him by the scruff.

'Stick it under the net,' he hissed, 'and, if you split, I'll flog the hide off you.'

The boy eeled into the bow pushing the heavy tin of tobacco ahead of him under the cross-benches. When it was safely buried he got back into the stern and clenched the oar again.

'Who's there?'

As the galley crept towards them, the old man raised his cracked voice in a salute of oaths. A tall man, in a pot-hat of varnished leather and a brass-buttoned stiff-collared coat, grappled the wherry with a boat-hook and swung the lantern over its occupants. Then he laughed and talked over his shoulder to the men in the boat with him.

'It's all right. It's only old Pa Smelley, out fishing again. Where you going tonight, Pa? You'll have to look slippy if you want to catch all them salmon coming up on the tide. The turn's at three o'clock. If you're not careful all the fish'll be up at Billingsgate afore you get there.'

The Peeler grinned at his joke. The old man was bowed down in the thwarts, swearing. The boy looked into the lantern with beady-eyed hate.

'Haven't you got nothing to say for yourself neither, son?'

'I ain't afeared of the likes of you. My Pa and me has got as much right on the river as you have.'

'You mind your tongue, you young mudlark. Go on, get along with the two of you. You might pick up a corpse and there's five nicker for you if you bring it in.'

He rocked the wherry with a vicious thrust of the boat-hook as the galley pulled away.

'It's all right, Pa. They're gone.'

'Lying bastards,' muttered the old man. 'Lying bastards, that's what they are. We didn't need no Peelers when we fished the river in the old days. No salmon, sez they. Before we had Peelers I've seen the river a-boil with them, Peter, when there were two 'undred boats working between Wandsworth and Gravesend. When I was a tiddler like you, in ole Fenimore's boat, we used to get five and six in a draw. There always was salmon in the Thames and there's salmon now. It's just netsman's luck that, lately, we haven't touched 'em. You marks my words, Peter. One night we'll have such a draught of salmon that we'll live like toffs for six months without working. We'll show 'em.'

The Peelers were right. Pa Smelley was dotty. Everybody on the riverside knew it, except Peter. He believed in him partly because he had nobody else to believe in, but also because he wanted to believe. More than anything else in the world, on those bitter nights when he helped to haul the net in his chilblained hands through the soured water, he wanted to believe.

' 'Ow will we know when we net a salmon, Pa?'

'You'll see his big black fin slicing through the water in the noose as the net closes in. Then you'll see the corks bob as he hits the mesh. That's the time when we pull long and slow and steady.'

'Where did you catch the most?'

'Where we're going tonight, Peter. Dead Man's Island, off the point. Down where, in the old days, the pirates used to dangle in their chains with their tallow dripping in the water. The danglers always drew the fish. I've had hundreds there, big uns too.'

'How long ago was that, Pa?'

'I ain't good at dates, Peter.'

' 'Ow long since you netted the last one?'

'I'm telling you, I ain't good at dates.'

' 'Ow do you know the salmon ain't all gone, same as Peg Weekes says?'

'What does Peg Weekes know? He ain't a netsman. I been a netsman all m'born days, and I'll die one.'

'Peg says it's them paddle-steamers what's done it. Drove all the fish out of the Thames, he sez.'

'It ain't because the fish ain't there anymore, it's because there ain't no netsmen anymore to catch 'em. 'Ow does anybody know they're all drove out when there's nobody to shoot a net for 'em when they run in? Nobody 'cept us. You and me is the only ones left of all the men and boys who used to work the River. Think of it, Peter. One night, tonight maybe, we'll make a strike again. Ten shillings a pound we'll get for 'em. Ten bob a pound at least.'

Peter edged the boat into the main current. Behind the pile of netting the old man stared out over the water. Darkness enveloped them on both banks. From Greenwich to Blackwall Point, to which they were drifting, the embankment was lined only with untamed vegetation, a few hulks and the marshland which, since Roman times, had spread over the Thames estuary.

'Peg Weekes,' Peter went on, 'sez you're balmy, Pa.'

'Peg Weekes sez he broached the rum cask they pickled Admiral Nelson in when they brought him back from Trafalgar. But it ain't true. They flogged him for eating tallow. You listen to your old Pa. You ain't called Peter for nothing. You're the grandson of your old Pa and I'll tell you

summat I ain't told nobody afore. I've seen the salmon
nights when you and me has been out together, Peter. What
do you say to that? I've seen 'em. I've heard 'em too. The
long splash when they're running. The heavy wallop when
they're sulking in the pool. I saw one jump once when you
was asleep in the boat. I was dozing myself. Then, suddenly,
he showed.'

'Was he a big 'un?'

'Twenty pounds, I reckon.'

'That's a whopper, Pa.'

'Garn, that's nothing for the Thames. They go thirty,
forty pounds in the spring run. Old Gatchet, him what died
of the yellow jack, he used to say this is a big river. And so
it is, Peter, so it is.'

As the old man wandered on in his dreamland, Peter
edged the boat across the current to the Kent side. The
iron-bound bow squelched into a tip of land which showed
at the ebb off the point between Blackwall Reach and
Bugsby's. Dropping over the side, he sank up to his calves
in the ooze lipping the water. The old man heaved a
grappling-iron after him. Staggering under the weight of the
iron hook, he skidded rather than walked, with the mooring
rope dragging behind him, up the foreshore.

At the flood, all that showed of Dead Man's Island was
a hump, little more than an eighth of an acre in area, overgrown with rank-smelling marsh plants. In the falling tide
it was nearly not an island at all. As Peter trod to the solid
ground above the tideway only a muddy shallow separated
the lump of land from the bank of the river.

Dropping the hook, he sank the spike into the spongy
soil. Then he went back to the boat.

The old man was hanging over the stern watching the

movement of a sliver of wood he had thrown on to the surface of the river. It drew slowly, but decisively, downstream.

'How is it, Pa?'

'Tide's still on the ebb. It'll be slack water in 'bout quarter of an hour.'

He passed the lantern and, wheezing with the strain, lowered himself from the boat.

'You can bring the baccy with you.'

The tin of tobacco, and the lantern as well, was almost more than Peter could carry. But, somehow, he managed it. As he stumbled through the soft stuff the glow of the lantern shed a faint circle of light about him. The surface below the high water mark was tinted red, red with the heads of millions of blood worms wriggling in the mud. On his way, his eyes lighted greedily on the rubbish left behind by the tide; remnants of copper and ironware, shreds of rope and lumps of clinker, clay pipes with broken stems, the refuse which no river, however wide or strong, could carry down to the sea.

Pa Smelley, too, was a remnant on the shore. He subsisted, he and Peter, on the pickings of the waterfront; on the pennies they could pick up ferrying people across the river; on the bits and pieces they salvaged in the mud at the ebb. He fed the faint flickers of vitality that still burned in him on the fuel of a hope that, one day, he would net a salmon again.

So it came about that, in the last hours of his life, he posted himself for the thousandth time against the rotting stump of what had once been a gibbet, waiting for the turn of the tide.

'Where's the baccy?'

When Peter handed him the tin, he dug it open with his jack-knife and cut off a plug.

'You're a good lad, Peter,' he commented as he turned the quid in his mouth, 'a good lad to your old Pa. I dunno what I should do without you. 'Ow much did you make today?'

'Tuppence for carrying beer cans down to the navvies what's working on the sewers in East-street. A mouldy for holding a swell's horse. And arf-a-mouldy for what I ain't telling you.'

'That's threepence halfpenny.'

'I spent a penny out of it on sausages.'

'What you want to waste money on them for? Didn't Polly have anything for you at the Fortune?'

'Only some chop bones. There was nothing on 'em.'

'You washed up, didn't you?'

'Customers was all hungry, Polly said. I ain't eaten much, Pa. Honest, I ain't.'

'Boys like you don't need it. What about your old Pa?'

'I got the baccy for you.'

'So you 'ave, so you 'ave. Sure you didn't trade any of it?'

'Haven't 'ad the chance,' said the boy simply.

'Don't worry, I won't bash you. You're a good boy at heart. Give me the tuppence halfpenny what's left and, if you do a proper night's work, I'll give you arf-a-mouldy back again for yourself.'

Peter handed over the money without question. Ever since he had haunted the narrow twisted lanes of the water-front, a little bare-foot urchin scavenging for what he could make or steal, Pa had taken the proceeds. It wasn't unfair. Only by pooling the pennies of the two of them could they collect the means to eat.

They lived together in a single room in a tumbledown

wooden tenement in a lane off the waterfront. The old man had an iron bedstead lined with straw-filled sacks; Peter rolled up on the floor. The two of them were lousy, illiterate and brutal. But, in their way, they were fond of each other. Neither of them had any other human beings to turn to.

Pa had told him that his mother, Pa's only daughter, had died when he was born. What he didn't tell him was that his mother had thrown herself into the river in the last stages of pregnancy; that she had been dragged out on a boat-hook and that she had died of a fever, shortly after he was born, which might have been anything because no doctor attended her.

In a vague uncomprehending way he associated his mother with the coming of the railway to Greenwich. He liked the railway. He loved the puffing engines, the steam, the furnaces and the noise. One day he went to the station and joined the other kids cartwheeling and somersaulting on the platform for pennies from the passengers. He brought home threepence. But, when he told Pa how he had earned it, the old man took off his leather belt and, ordering him to let down his trousers, he thrashed his narrow rump until he fell fainting on the floor. All he knew, when it was over, was that he must never go to the railway again. He asked Peg Weekes about it. And Peg Weekes tried to tell him why.

Peg Weekes was his hero. He was a Jack Collegeman, one of the old tars who were pensioners in the Greenwich Hospital. Peg had lost a leg in the wars. His favourite boast was that after the battle of Trafalgar he had been flogged for tapping the rum cask in which they brought Nelson home to England. He loved to show the criss-cross scars on his back where the bos'un's cat-o-ninetails had licked him.

And although, on the waterfront, they said that the flogging he had taken had made him light in the head, Peter at any rate believed everything that Peg told him; excepting, of course, that his Pa, too, was balmy.

When he asked Peg about the railway, Peg said—because he didn't know any other way of expressing himself—that his mother had got herself into the family way with one of those swell Cockneys; that's why she threw herself into the river. Peter was troubled, not because he understood what Peg was talking about—he didn't—but because it confirmed in his mind the belief that the railway was a wicked thing. Although it fascinated him, he kept away.

It was easier for him to keep away from the trains now that, in the streets of Greenwich, there was the counter-attraction of the construction of the new sewer. Four winding engines, steaming deliciously, were employed to pull up and tip into carts the excavated soil; and, day and night, two pumping engines were coughing up water, a fascinating spectacle to him and every urchin in the district.

Most mornings, he was can-boy to the navvies. In middle-day, he helped Polly, who was a barmaid at the public house named the 'Fortune of War.' Polly had wet-nursed him, for a penny a day, when he was a baby. In her way, she loved him.

In his way, too, he was happy. He swam like a sewer rat. He hated Peelers; and it was his pride that he could outwit them. He watched the sideshows, especially the dancing bears which enchanted him, without paying. He fought the butchers' boys. He raided the barges moored in the tideway. And, every now and then, he went out on these strange expeditions, for the fish that weren't there, with his Pa.

He never reasoned it out. Pa had a boat. Pa was so old

that, whatever anybody said, Pa must know what he was talking about.

How he talked.

'Ignoramuses,' he said.

'What's that, Pa?'

'Like what it says in the Bible. The unbelievers, Peter, shall perish in hell fire.'

'Is that like the railway?'

'What's the railway got to do with it? I'm telling you, Peter. Nobody believed in Jonah and the Whale till the whale swallowed him. Everybody what knows nothing says there are no salmon left no more in the Thames. Do you believe that, Peter?'

'No, Pa, not if you sez so.'

'Then go down and say how the tide's running; and don't waste your time picking up rubbish.'

Obediently, Peter carried the lantern to the tideline. He had done just that so many times before. To shoot and draw a seine in the strong waters of the Thames was only possible in the slack at the bottom of the ebb and at the top of the flood.

Peter looked steadfastly at the river. The wherry, which had been pulling down-current on the mooring rope, was rocking indeterminately in midstream. From Gravesend to Teddington Lock every craft in the crowded waterlane of London was moving restlessly, awaiting the thrust of the new tide. In Westminster, people stirred in their beds as Big Ben spoke the hour and then, inexplicably, boomed seventeen times more.

'Tide's at the slack, Pa.'

With a satisfied grunt, the old man went to the boat and,

leaning heavily over the side, heaved out the head-rope. Pulling the warp up the mud, he made it fast against the post he had been leaning on.

Peter held the wherry steady while the old man clambered aboard. Then, doubling his frail frame with the effort, striving with head and arms and skinny loins, he pushed off and, splashing through the water, leant over the side and twisted himself into the boat on the axis of his belly button.

This time the old man rowed, crouched bat-like on the cross-bench in the middle of the wherry with two long oars licking the water. He pulled stern-first at an up-river angle as Peter freed the seine. A line of corks, rolling in the wake of the boat, stretched away from his busy hands. Towards the Essex side of the river, the last cork jumped overboard. Sixty fathoms of net were set. The old man turned the bow across the river and called Peter to take an oar; the two of them rowed side by side in a wide arc down-river and across the stream again.

Sluggishly, reluctantly, the bobbing chain of corks tightened into a horseshoe behind them. The purse of the net slowly closed. When they had fallen a little below the island, the old man gave Peter a nudge to pull inshore. Straining on the oars, they grounded the boat about fifteen yards below the point where the head of the net was dragging on the post.

The tide was turning; but not yet enough to make a distinctive change in the flow of the current. The old man noted the new mark on the foreshore with satisfaction. It was the exact time when the pressure of the fresh water coming down the river would meet the surge of the sea as it started to roll in against it; the time, when the head of water was lifting, that a fish waiting in the estuary would have felt the urge to run.

He cut himself another quid of tobacco from the tin. Peter heaved while he waited but the seine was too heavy for him to move alone. The half-dozen corks nearest to him bobbed derisively in the water. The net, sensitive to the first pull of the tide, narrowed into a long upstream loop.

'Time to make the draw,' said the old man. 'Have you said your prayers, Peter?'

'Not yet, Pa.'

'Then start now, you . . . How do you expect to net fish if you ain't religious, same as I've told you? Go on, pray while we heave.'

With a zeal that was almost fanatical the old man bent to the haul. Peter caught hold of the ropes to assist his Pa. The net started to move slowly in the water as, with shrill voice, the child parroted, 'Our Father what art in Heaven . . .' and paused.

'Go on, you ain't got started yet.'

'I've forgotten the words, Pa.'

'Ain't I learnt you proper? Go on, or I'll give you the end of the warp.'

'Forgive us this day our daily bread . . . Is that right, Pa?'

'That'll do, but keep at it and mind you watch the net.'

Hand over hand, they coiled the ropes into the mud and brought in the two wings of the seine. When the noose was closed the old man checked the draw of the foot-rope to make sure that it was pulling tighter than the head. It was essential to bring in the net so that it bagged from the bottom, closing any possibility of escape. When he was satisfied, he put his back again into the labour of hauling.

As the purse got smaller it moved more easily through

the water. Peter went on singing jumbled phrases from the Lord's prayer. The old man himself mumbled bits of hymns and mixed-up passages out of the Bible. But as the net closed Peter dried into silence. He peered into the necklace of corks for a glimpse of that black fin slicing the water that he had been told to look for so many times before.

'What's come over you? Why aren't you prayin'?'

The old man almost screamed it as, with fierce energy, he laid into the last of the work. Under the driving pressure, the corks ducked-and-draked in the water. Peter, endeavouring to keep up with the old man, half keeled over.

'Can't think of any more words to pray with, Pa.'

'Then go on spoutin' what you've been spouting already. Holy Mary, Mother o' God . . . go on, blast you.'

The seine closed into a small tight circle. Peter bumbled words into the night that he didn't understand while, with a bloodshot glint in his eye, the old man sweated over him and the two of them stood to the side of a growing pile of netting.

The end of the net bellied upstream as the new tide began to press more insistently into the river. If a fish was lying quiet in the purse, it was the moment when he could be expected to show.

All that showed, as they dragged the bag ashore, was a swollen black bundle which slopped wetly in the end of it. The old man picked it out from the lip of the water and stared at it unbelievingly. It was a dead cat, and stinking.

At the full length of his arm, he swung it back into the river. Then he turned on Peter, who was bending over the heaped seine, and knocked him off his feet with a cuff of the back of his hand.

'You didn't pray proper, you didn't pray.'

He stumbled abstractedly up what was left of the fore-shore and squatted down, in lonely misery, on the hump of the island. Peter, recovering his feet, pressed his burning ear and snivelled gently to himself.

He didn't feel any resentment towards his Pa; but towards the river. If the river only yielded dead cats, Pa was simply taking out of him what the river was taking out of Pa.

He shook out the net, fold by fold, and settled it into the boat again. It was monstrously heavy work for a boy but Pa had put him to it ever since he could remember. In the small hours of the night, in the star-starved darkness, the starveling did a man's job with leaden arms and eyes that fought with his knuckles with weariness.

It was only when the net was safely stowed that he re-joined his Pa. The old man was sleeping; or, rather, his eyes were closed in the semi-consciousness which, at great age, passes for sleep. Peter squatted on his narrow hunkers beside him and locked his arms about his drawn-up knees. His head dropped forward and, almost at once, he slept fast.

He was awakened by the old man shaking him violently by the shoulder.

'Wake up, boy, wake up, can't you?'

'What's the matter, Pa?'

He stirred himself with a shiver. Blinking, he looked into the dove-grey and lemon light of a winter's morning.

'I ain't imagining it, Peter. I know I ain't. I've seen 'im, I tell you. Out there, 'bout twenty yards off the point.'

For a moment or two, Peter was still too full of sleep to comprehend. He stared vaguely about him. The tide was rising to the full, the wherry swam way out in the stream, and the hump of land they sat on had shrunk into a pimple on the river's surface.

'Keep your young eyes on the river out there, Peter. He'll show again as sure as God made you. You believe me, don't you, Peter? I've seen him. I knowed I've seen him. I can't have dreamed it, can I? Not this time.'

The old man clutched Peter's arm in a fierce grip. He was trembling, but not with cold; and there was a despairing appeal in his voice.

'What you seen, Pa?'

'What do you think I've seen? A salmon, Peter.'

'A big 'un?'

'Big as Jonah's whale, boy. Out there, where the stream shelves down into the deep run. That's where they always lie when they're runnin'. Where the current's deep and fast. Are you watching? Just tell me, boy, that your ole Pa's lamps ain't played 'im false.'

'Can't see nothing, Pa.'

'You will, Peter, you will.'

Peter rubbed the sleep out of his eyes and stared into the steely-mirrored surface where his Pa had pointed. His arm was numb with the grasp that the old man kept on him. His belly was retching with hunger. His knees were knocking with cold.

For a time, the two of them stared at the water in silence. And then the miracle happened. A silver shape, iridescent with flashing pinks and blues and greens, rose out of the Thames like the blade of Excalibur. It was a straight upward leap, a leap of distress; but, for a moment, the salmon hung clear of the water. Then, with a great splash, he settled into the stream again.

II

AN OLD MAN'S DREAM

As the fish showed the old man emitted a weird cry, a sound like a mourner at a wake, an involuntary moan that squeezed out of his lungs as if he had encountered a ghost or sighted the image of his own fate in the looking-glass of the river. He rocked his head from side to side in a sort of trance while Peter, eyes bright with interrogation, looked at him wonderingly.

'What's the matter, Pa?'

The old man stared into the air with wooden-faced detachment.

'Are you all right, Pa?'

There was a note of alarm in the question which penetrated the old man's consciousness.

'It's m'head, Peter. It'll pass off. I keeps on seeing things.'

'I saw him too, Pa. He looked like what you always said he would. Ain't he a real one?'

An expression of cunning revealed itself in the watery pupils of the old man's eyes.

'What did you see? Don't lie to me. What did you see?'

'Same as you said. Jumped clean out of the water he did with the spray rolling off his back. He was bigger than a cod what you see in the fishmonger's and he was silver all over like a new tanner.'

'You wouldn't say that to your old Pa if it weren't true, would you, Peter? Or would you?'

He twisted Peter's arm in a talon grip.

'You're hurting me.'

'T'ain't nothing to what I'll do to you if you're lying. Where was he?'

Peter pointed.

'Out there, where you said, off the shelf.'

'That's where he'd be, if he's there.'

'But I've seen 'im, Pa.'

'And you ain't seen one afore, 'ave you, Peter? Not like me when I were a nipper in ole Fenimore's boat. We took hundreds every season, harvest cocks and big 'uns, too.'

'This one's a big 'un, Pa.'

'That's what I said,' muttered the old man vaguely.

'Ain't we going to make a draw for 'im?'

'Summat's bangin' in m'head, Peter.'

'If we shoot 'arf the net we can get him.'

'I've been on the nets when we've taken six or seven in a draw. That's not counting shad and smelt. Times the market was so glutted with salmon you couldn't give 'em away. So many of 'em it wasn't worth stopping up the holes in the seine.'

The old man's voice faded into an incomprehensible mumble. The grip that he had kept on Peter's arm relaxed. His head dropped forward and, apart from the movement of his lips, he stiffened into a torpor.

Peter tried to rouse him. He might as well have tried to refloat one of the hulks glued into the silt of the tideway. The old man looked the way he looked when he was drunk;

but he wasn't drunk. He had watched him too often, the white tip of his nose pressed on the frosted glass windows of riverside gin palaces, to be mistaken about that. He supposed that Pa was angry with him—perhaps because he hadn't prayed hard enough—but it was not the way that he had ever taken it out of him before. The immobility of the old man puzzled him. He felt lonely and bewildered.

Self-reliant urchin that necessity had made him, he was still a small boy; as apt to tears as other boys, as quick to panic in a strange situation as any little lord in a lace collar without somebody to hold his hand. If only Pa would just hit him, the way he always did, instead of acting as if he couldn't hear or see.

With a matchstick of an arm wrapped about the old man's shoulders he rose to his knees and searched the river. A chilly mist blanketed the water; the light was fog-grey. Somewhere downstream, a paddle-steamer sounded her siren; but the reaches above and below the island were deserted. There were no wayfarers on the overgrown path alongside the embankment. The tide, curling round Dead Man's Island, ringed him off from the outside world in a flood of chill indifference.

In the ordinary way, if he had sighted anyone on the bank or a craft on the water, he would have ducked for cover. He had long since discovered that boys like him were regarded by most grown-ups as natural enemies, objects to be chivvied and cuffed and chased. But the emptiness of the river for once emphasised the emptiness inside him.

With all the abandon of his thirteen years, he exploded into tears. A passing black-headed gull screamed a protest; but the old man under his pot-hat never as much as stirred.

In the mist of his misery he had forgotten the fish. When the salmon rose again, twisting in discomfort on the surface as he gasped for oxygen in the polluted water, it was the splash as he plunged that arrested his attention. Wiping the wet out of his eyes with the back of his hand he watched the swelling rings rippling out over the lie. The snivel dried in his nose.

With a leaping heart he looked once more to the old man for guidance. But it was only a glance. The call of the fish, resplendent with life, was stronger than anything he had ever known. He couldn't wait.

He went to the water's edge and, sinking on hands and knees, with his tail cocked in the air, hung over the black face of the river as if by closing the distance between himself and the salmon he could draw nearer to possessing it. More than anything else that he had ever desired he wanted to make that bar of silver his own.

As long as he could remember, the sheer existence of such a creature had been an object of faith with him; the symbol, branded into his impressionable mind by his Pa, of the unattainable. It represented wealth, and truth, and beauty. And it was waiting there almost within reach of his arms.

He had never heard of miracles. Nothing that he had ever had in life had been won without a struggle. The salmon was a thing to lay his hands on like a chop off a butcher's boy's stretcher or a box of lucifers when the grocer was looking the other way. He sat back on his heels and scouted warily up and down the river. Behind him, on the island, the figure of the old man was outlined against the morning sky like a tombstone; otherwise, the coast was empty.

He crept along the water's edge to the rope mooring the

wherry. Heaving gently, with quick checks over his shoulder to make sure that Pa wasn't stirring, he eased the boat out of the stream up to the flood-tide mark.

Following the old man's example, he tossed a fragment of driftwood into the current. It circled round without direction. He had instinctively sensed the vital fifteen minutes when the tide was hovering on the turn again.

He had never shot a net alone. Only boyish recklessness tempted him now. Very quietly, he lowered the mooring-rope and its iron into the bow. Dragging on the heavy warp of the seine, he lashed it with inherited skill to the broken post on the island. Then he clambered into the boat and humped a heap of the net over the side.

When he sat down on the cross-bench to man the oars he had to make a struggle to raise the blades. But he stretched his legs to the toes to gain a foothold and, as he pulled, he carried back the leather-shod handles to his ears. Feathering the water, he floated the weight of the paddles on the river as he bent forward and pulled with a quick lick, exactly the length of his arms, as he leant back.

With the weight of the seine leaning against the weight of the boat, he could only move slowly; but, in the slack water, he crept steadily away from the island. The net that he had heaped on the bank unfolded behind him. Shipping the oars, he clambered forward and shook out some more. The corks settled in a close-packed bundle, but the first five fathoms were away.

Rowing steadily under the arch of the long blades, he pressed on until, once again, the drag of the net checked all movement in the boat. Patiently, he unloaded another length and, stubbornly, pulled out the web behind him. He was attempting something which, theoretically, was beyond his strength; he was achieving it with a mixture of urchin-cunning and a quality which, in a better-brought-up child, would have been called heroism. The cunning that he had learnt in a lifetime on the waterfront was more important. He knew the ways of the river; he recognised that he was battling against time and tide.

Unless he could clear the seine before the ebb gathered force, the odds were that he would lose the net and fall well below Dead Man's Island before he could ease the boat into the bank. In that event he was under no illusions as to what the reckoning would be with Pa. But nothing that he had ever undertaken had been free of the threat of reprisal if he was caught.

He didn't bother his head with what the future might hold if he failed. His whole present being was concentrated in his determination to ring the net about the salmon; some-how, to make the thing his own.

Aware where it lay, he made no attempt to stretch the seine over a large surface of water. He kept the boat heading into the river against the strain of the obstinate corks until the movement under his seat warned him that the tide was starting to ebb again. He brought the oars inboard and, allowing the wherry to drift, tumbled the heart of the net overboard.

He worked quick: but not quickly enough. The speed of the drift accelerated and, when he leant breathlessly on the oars to edge into the bank, he hadn't the muscle to pull straight across the stream to the island. The current carried the wherry relentlessly past it and the best he could do was to guide it into the overgrown herbage of the main river bank below.

But he had the net; the end was securely lashed to the

plank of the cross-bench. As the boat bounced into the bank
he dived into the bow for the mooring-rope and got ashore.
He scrambled through the clinging hug of the weeds on to
the tow-path. Taking a bearing, he hung the mooring-rope
over his shoulder and, bowing his back, dragged against the
stream.

The wherry pushed her bow obstinately into every
wrinkle in the embankment. He eased her off and coaxed
her through the easy shallows on the edge of the current.
He brought her up the river until she bounced ill-temperedly
in the channel dividing the island from the main bank. What
he had already done, although he didn't think about it, was
a considerable achievement.

The stream in the dividing gut of water was moving too
fast for him to haul the boat further upstream. He had
carried it, with the wing of the seine fighting astern, nearly
fifty yards. A forlorn figure, he gazed towards the island.

The channel, at high water, was little more than twenty
yards wide, and most of it was shallow; but, single-handed,
he couldn't expect to get the boat across the fast water for
another hour or two.

The net, under the developing pull of the tide, had settled
in a downstream bag. But, at the Bugsby's Reach end of the
island, a snag had checked it. It lay like the letter 'W,'
bellying in the outside curve, nipping the tip of a mudbank
in the middle, and swinging away again in a narrower arc
in the channel between the restless stern of the wherry and
the miserable scrap of land beyond.

Peter measured the situation, and made his decision. Many
times, he had had a tougher job to board a mere barge. He
threw the square of hopsack off his head and slipped out of
the ragged pea-jacket which he had inherited from Pa. Roll-

ing the stuff into a bundle he buried it, at a safe distance
from the footpath, among the rank tufts of the reeds.

Half naked, he slid fearlessly down the bank into the icy
water. Gripping the side of the wherry he got a foothold
on the mud. Then he closed his hands on the rough warp of
the seine and dragged himself, hand over hand, into the
channel. The current tossed him like an empty bottle. The
rope sank under his weight as if it wanted to drown him.
The river clung about his limbs trying to freeze him. But,
although he was blue with cold and fighting for the comfort
of mere breath, he had the wriggle of an elver. Head down
in the water, he battled his way, inch by inch, across the
channel.

The net treated him as if he was an enemy. It ducked
and rolled and tried to sweep away from him in the kick of
the tide; but he stuck on. He was underwater when he
closed his fingers into the knots of the mesh. Bursting his
ribs, he clawed to the surface and hung, keeled over the
head-rope, in a mob of quarrelling corks.

He was dead-beat. His cramped hands let go of the net.
He slipped into the ooze almost thankfully. Almost as if he
preferred to be drowned. But, as he gave up the struggle,
his feet found bottom. Leaning into the embrace of the
seine, dragging in a muddy spillikins round his ankles, he
recovered his breath. He had carved his way through the
current to the point where the net was snagged. Turning
about, he blundered through the shallow water on to dry
land.

He had defeated death by the mere chance that the push
of the tide had raised the level of the head of silt off the
end of the island. Shaking himself, he squeezed the water out
of his rags and paddled towards the old man.

Pa was bunched under his pot-hat and mildewed sea-cloak in the same frozen posture in which he had left him; like a cormorant drooping its wings on its perch on the water's edge.

'I've shot the net, Pa.'

For answer the old man moaned quietly to himself.

'I said I shot the net, Pa.'

He peered under the chimney of the tall hat and earnestly examined the blue-veined and white-stubbled face underneath it.

'Why ain't you talkin' to me, Pa? I ain't done nothing wrong. I ain't lost the net. I shot it good.'

His teeth chattered as he talked. His wet clothes clung to his carcass like streamers of flannel-weed. Blue with cold he pressed closer to the old man. Then, venturingly, he lifted the hair blanket off Pa's shoulders and wrapped it round his own. The old man didn't seem to mind; he didn't seem to mind anything anymore.

Hugging the blanket about him his attention was distracted by the chug of a tug-boat steaming up the river. Paddles flaying it came into view with a train of barges wallowing heavily behind it. He shook the old man's shoulder and jumped up and down in agitation.

'The net's out, Pa. They'll cut the net.'

Stirring a little in his coma, the old man vaguely pushed him away. Peter ran to the warp and, laying his puny weight against the cable, tried to heave. The seine scarcely moved. He had set it alone; alone he knew that he was powerless to haul it.

It was only then that the possibility that Pa wasn't behaving the way he was just because he was feeling narky dawned in his mind. Until the tug swung out to round the point he had simply supposed that Pa was in one of his moods; one of those unpredictable tantrums which made people say that he was balmy. But Pa wasn't the sort of balmy who would sit there, moaning and groaning, while a paddle-steamer chewed up the net. Earlier he had felt frightened and lonely without realising why. Now, he looked again at the crouching figure behind him with fearful understanding. He had no comprehension of death; but, instinctively, he recoiled from the mystery of it.

He wanted to run away; but there was nowhere to run away to. He yearned to bury his head somewhere; somewhere warm and yielding like Polly's lap. The tug, which had seemed so hostile, became a friendly thing; something that pulsed and moved in the emptiness that enveloped him.

As it bustled round the bend in the river he caught a glimpse of a bearded face inside the wheelhouse. Windmilling his arms, dancing on the water's edge, he tried to be noticed. The skipper peered curiously through the glass of the cabin at the frog hopping about on the mudbank. Then his eye lighted on the ring of corks swaying in the channel. He spun the wheel and the train of boats drew away from the island to make a wider arc of the reach.

In the stern of the last of them, a bargee sat in a chair gravely smoking a long churchwarden clay pipe. Peter, in his desolation, cupped his hands to his mouth to holler him. But, as he drew breath, it was knocked out of him by another startling splash in the water. The salmon was stirring again.

His eyes darted from the barges drawing away like black monsters into the mist, and settled on the bursting rings over the fish's lie. But only fleetingly.

Behind him, unbelievably, the old man was stirring, too

As if in answer to the summons of the fish he was seized with a sudden paroxysm of coughing. Clawing at the marsh grass, he started to drag himself to his feet.

'Pa!'

Peter made impulsively towards him; then checked in his tracks. The old man's eyes were looking without seeing. He was standing up mechanically on muscles that were working without mind.

With a fixed stare, he brushed past his grandson and stumbled to the river's edge. Automatically, he laid hold of the warp of the net and tested the pressure of the tide. Then he unlashed it from the post and hauled. Although his face was a mask, he eased in a couple of fathoms of cable as if he could feel in his arms that the seine was snagged. Peter crept close behind him and watched what went on with beady attention. It was fortunate that he did.

The old man let the warp drop out of his hands. Shambling across the mud, he made off to find the other wing of the net. Under the pull of the ebb, the cable snaked back into the water. Peter grabbed it.

He couldn't recover what had been lost already; he couldn't even hold the net where it lay. Giving way step by step, all he could manage was to control the downward drift, to hold the purse above the salmon's lie before Pa came back. As the minutes rolled by, the pull of the stream grew stronger. The weight on the seine increased slowly, but inexorably. At last, his feet slipped from underneath him. The warp seared through his hands and he came down on his back in the mud.

He had all but lost the fight when a powerful heave behind him lifted him on to his legs again. The net ducked obstinately, and checked, under the renewed pressure. Peter scrambled clear as Pa, a dumb spectre, spread his legs and heaved.

The other wing of the seine was at his feet. Somehow he had clawed it out of the ˜silt; somehow he had knifed off enough of the warp, its head tied to the wherry on the other side of the channel, to centre the two ends. Gathering them together, he closed the noose.

The drag of the tide made him grunt with effort. Two thin streams of saliva trickled from his lips. His eyes were glazed and rheumy; and he was incapable of speech. But habit ruled his muscles, and what was left of his mind. He hauled on the downstream bag easing the other wing against it until the seine was evenly balanced in the stream.

'Our Father what art in Heaven . . .'

Peter dragged at the mesh as Pa brought it in, reckless of the untidy heap that was gathering about his feet. He stumbled in it, he knelt in it, he hacked his shin-bones in his excitement on the leads as he sang out inconsequential bits of prayer.

The seine was closing round the salmon's lie. The draw was getting easier. The old man got well down so that the pressure came from the level of his knees. He pulled slowly, floating-in the corks with scarcely a ripple and keeping the leads hugging the bottom. The longer the salmon was un-suspecting the surer the catch. The steadier the final draw the less chance there was of his slipping under the net, or over it.

The muck of the Thames rolled out of the mesh over the old man's arms and legs. Peter knelt in the heap of netting gazing tensely into the oval of the black water framed in the yellow corks. The frame was growing very small.

If the fish was there he must show soon. No salmon, as

big as this one was, was likely to lay quiet. The possibility
that the seine might have missed him was becoming unbear-
able. Peter, his face twisted with anxiety, looked pleadingly
to his Pa for hope. No emotion of any kind showed in the
old man's features.

But deep down inside him, as he fluttered between life
and oblivion, he must have known. He worked the seine as
if, through the clouded crystals of his eyes, he could see
things that the boy couldn't. He looked the way that Lazarus
must have looked when he rose from the tomb. He acted as
if he had been turned back from eternity to fulfil some fearful purpose.

He steadied the net, balancing the two ends in outspread
arms, sooner than any normal netsman could have anticipated the first driving rush of the fish. With a sudden swirl,
a black fin curved a V-shaped wave across the purse. The
old man slacked the net to meet him as he hit it; forty
pounds of silver vigour, powered by panic, irritated to
madness by the stifling water in which he was trying to
breathe. The ring of corks dipped deep in salute as he
torpedoed into the embrace of the mesh. Then the corks
bobbed to the surface again as, with a flash of his spade tail,
he freed himself from the clinging bag and made a rush for
a break-through in another direction.

Peter was leaping up and down in the mud, shouting with
exultation. The old man, the line of his pot-hat almost
horizontal with the water, was silently nursing-in the last
few fathoms of the seine.

The salmon, baulked in the oval belly of it, thrashed
about purposelessly in the tail. The vibrating energy that
he had brought with him from the sea was seeping out of
him. The lack of oxygen in the stream stifled his breathing.

He sank back and lay exhausted between the folds of the
mesh.

'There he is, Pa, there he is!'

Peter screamed in his excitement. Tearing at the net, he
went down on his knees as the old man ran the salmon
ashore. Flapping weakly, it lay hammocked in the dirty
shroud; a creature of wondrous beauty whose hog-back,
even in the smoky reaches of the lower Thames, reflected
every subtle colour in the spectrum.

Unbelievingly, Peter put out his hand to touch it. The
old man dropped the seine and made as if it was his intention to lift the salmon out of the net. Instead, he took a few
faltering paces and then reeled on his heels on the river's
edge.

'Peter,' he said, 'I'm going.'

As he looked up from the fish, the old man fell back into
the river. In his dying convulsion he got a hand to the heap
of netting. Twisting his fingers into it, his fist closed in the
grip of death. As his body was carried off by the current,
the net started to slip away, fold after fold, behind it.

For a moment, all that Peter took in was Pa's pot-hat
bobbing emptily in the river. In panic, he tried to check
the escaping seine; but, with every fathom, it was gathering
momentum. He looked distractedly about him to see what
he should do. His eyes fell on the salmon, still wrapped in
the net which Pa was relentlessly dragging downstream with
him.

Throwing himself on the fish, he fumbled to find a way
into the bag. The head- and heel-ropes had got entangled.
The hemp of the net itself defied him when he tried to break
it. He picked up a broken bottle in the mud and started
laboriously to saw through the tarred string. All the time,

Pa was taking more and more of the net away with him. In his anguish, he hated Pa.

Wrapping his arms about the salmon inside the net, he dragged it further from the water's edge. It was a waste of effort if he couldn't free the fish, but it seemed to make it more his own. Then, as he struggled, he saw a glint of something half buried in the mud. It was Pa's jack-knife, lying there almost as if Pa had meant him to find it.

Tearing out the blade with the tips of his nails, he slashed at the mesh. He ripped it sufficiently to wrap his two hands round the root of the salmon's broad tail. He pulled the fish clear as the net slithered away down the mudbank after Pa.

In his joy he hugged the creature to his heart. Then, giddy with excitement and exhaustion, convulsed between laughter and tears, he swam into unconsciousness.

III

THE SONG THAT WAS FALSE

As he slept, the flow of the current between the island and the bank ebbed to a dribble; the wherry keeled over in the mud.

Through the murk on the Essex side the sun broke through like a muffled lantern. In the main stream, the penny steamers—the bus service of the Thames—began their daily chore; plying up and down between the landing-stages spaced from Westminster to Gravesend. Barges and small craft drifted about their business. Tugs, with twin funnels laid side by side, smoked industriously as they nuzzled the hulls and dragged at the bows of ocean-going sailing vessels. The river heaved and foamed, the pumps of the ships vomited, in the day-time traffic of the most crowded waterway in the world.

Not one of the bonneted and top-hatted passengers crowding the decks of the paddle-boats manifested any interest in the bundle curled on the tide-line. Ragged children were too familiar to merit attention. The markets, the street corners and the docks were infested with them; unwanted brats grown in worldly cunning out of all keeping with their years and with a capacity for making a nuisance of themselves out of all proportion to their size.

How long he slept Peter didn't know. He was roused by
the siren of a passing steamer. In half wakefulness, he looked
about for the shambling familiar figure of Pa. Then he
remembered the salmon. It lay, mud-stained but lovely in
death at his side, half buried under the hair blanket which
he had lifted off Pa's shoulders. As if to reassure himself,
he touched the scars on its flanks where the scales had
been rubbed off in its struggle in the net. He opened the
beak of its mouth and felt the needles of its teeth. He stared
at the colours that irradiated the mailed silver of its
body.

The salmon was a cock fish who had been away many
years on the ocean feeding-banks but it was unlikely that he
had been spawned in the Thames. Destiny had urged him up
the lower reaches of a river to which he did not belong; a
soured waterway to which no fish belonged anymore. Or
fishermen. Pa, the last of them, had gone.

But Peter had the fish. In the fever of possession, it seemed
a good exchange. If Pa was there he would have taken the
salmon away from him. He had no thought of what he was
going to do with his prize, or what use it could be to him.
Living for the moment, he gloated over the thing from the
sea that was all his.

With the instinct of a wild thing over a kill—he was
nearly that—he sensed rather than sighted the four-oared
police galley among the other craft rounding the reach. At
once, with the certainty of self-preservation, he knew that
they were after him. Maybe one of the paddle-boats had
fouled the net and reported it. Maybe somebody down
river had grappled a hook into Pa's corpse. He never
doubted that, if the Peelers copped him, they would take
away the fish and give him a whipping for good measure,

too. Boys like him couldn't expect any other treatment.
They just hid themselves, while they could.

He glanced at the bank. The marshland was as deserted
as it had been in the night. At any time, only a few
pedestrians used the path along the river between Greenwich
and Woolwich. Beyond the embankment, huge rhubarb-like
plants and rank weeds rose in a tangled jungle. It was where
he had hidden his jacket.

Taking the salmon's tail with both hands, he half lifted
it. He wasn't tall enough to raise it off the ground. He
dragged it, as an otter would, over the hump of the island
and sledged it through the slush left behind by the falling
tide. Ducking under the shelter of the wherry, he stopped
for breath. The police galley was still well up-river, and
rowing slowly.

They hadn't spotted him; but it wouldn't be long before
they discovered Pa's boat. He had to get the fish as far away
from the boat as he could manage.

He hadn't realised how heavy it was, and he hadn't
reckoned on raising it on to the embankment. By clinging
to the bunches of reed, he could shin up easily enough by
himself; but not with the slippery fish as well. He cast about
for a solution. The police galley was drawing nearer.

He half covered the fish with mud. Then, climbing on
to the bow thwart of the wherry he scrambled up the
mooring-rope on to the footpath. He raised the hook that
held it and hung it over the bank. With his heart thumping
with the exertion, he slid back on to the river bed. Drawing
the rusty iron towards the salmon, he twisted the hook into
the fish's gills and out of its mouth. Too fearful to look
behind him, he again scaled the embankment and, lying on
his face, gathered the rope in both fists and pulled.

He could hear the rhythmic splash of the Peelers' oars as, hand over hand, he gently dragged the fish towards him. The cumbrous shape of the mooring-hook snagged in the tall weeds. At any moment he expected a figure in a leather pot-hat to rise up and snatch the salmon off the end of it. Now he could hear the Peelers talking together. Recklessly, he dragged in the last few yards of the rope. The weeds parted and the fish was at his feet.

Taking it off the hook, he got both arms underneath it and, bent in half, staggered with it in a sort of falling run across the footpath into the tall cover of the marsh.

On the greasy ground he slipped, and the fish slithered ahead of him into the undergrowth. For a moment or two, he lay quite still; then he raised his head and listened. When he was quite satisfied that the Peelers weren't on his tail, he crawled towards the salmon.

He dragged it into the deepest reed bed that he could find, where the marsh squelched underfoot and the bruised undergrowth had an aromatic oniony smell. He at last felt safe. But he also knew that he could go no further alone. He started to miss Pa. He wanted Polly, or Peg Weekes, to find him so that he could tell them about it. Thinking of Polly made him think how hungry he was.

He squatted beside the salmon, his arms wrapped round his up-drawn knees, because it was warmer that way, until he could sit still no longer. Then he carefully hid the fish under a covering of coarse grass. He crept on to the foot-path and, parting the herbage on the embankment, peered over the river's edge. The Peelers had gone: so had Pa's boat. He could see the track in the mud made by the iron keel where they had shoved the wherry into the water.

Boldly now, he went to the place where he had rolled up

his jacket and his hopsack hood. He piled his wretched rags on his back, and turned towards the footpath. As he neared the embankment, a sound checked him.

On that dreary March morning a song-bird was trilling. Restlessly, insistently, apparently endlessly, it piped its call. And, as it piped, the note grew steadily shriller and nearer.

The bird was in a cage, balanced on the top of a pile of hampers in a hand-barrow. A gypsy-looking man was pushing the barrow along the track towards Greenwich. He wore a dirty smock-frock—he had no shirt—and his long black hair trailed under a wide-brimmed soft hat with a tall sugar-loaf crown. Like Peter, he was barefooted and unwashed.

He was a wild-bird catcher, bringing in his bag to hawk it in the streets of Greenwich.

The bird which was singing was a mule—a cross between a goldfinch and a canary—trained to call incessantly and so beguile the wild birds into the net. The net, with the four iron pins used to set it, lay on the barrow. In the hampers, beating their wings in terror against the cane bars, was the catch—cock linnets, starlings, finches, redbreasts, throstles, blackbirds—every species that the call-bird could mock into the snare.

Peter, like other boys, was fascinated by the bird-catchers. Once one of them had given him a starling, it was almost dead when he got it—braced with tapes on the end of a stick so that it looked tame. The piping of the call-bird attracted him, as he stood in the cover of the reeds, as it attracted the victims of its own kind.

He whistled a tune in answer. Blowing all he knew, he hooked his fingers under his armpits and, adopting a cheeky

Cockney swagger, sauntered on to the footpath. The ritual of the London streets, in striking an acquaintanceship or measuring an adversary, was an established one. It was based on a preliminary reconnaissance, distinguished on both sides by an affection of complete disinterest. As he strolled on to the footpath, Peter gave no hint that he was aware of the bird-catcher's presence at all. His head was in the air whistling madly. But, with every step, he reduced his pace until the creaking barrow with its mocking call-bird was just behind him. Then, with a casual roll, he stepped aside to let it pass.

'Catched much, mister?'

'You 'op it.'

The bird-catcher put down the barrow and eyed him suspiciously.

'What you bin up to?'

'I ain't done nothing.'

'You bin up to something. Must 'ave. And you let them linnets be.'

Peter quickly withdrew a finger which he had casually poked between the cane bars of one of the fluttering hampers of birds. In silence, the bird-catcher resettled the load on the barrow.

He carried his head as if it were too heavy for him, with averted eyes. He skulked, when he moved, like a fox. When he spoke, it was as if a moth was speaking; his voice was so quiet. Peter whistled up his courage.

'Want to do yourself a bit o' good, mister?'

The bird-catcher indicated his interest by moving his head slowly from side to side; but he didn't say anything.

'Maybe I can put you in the way of a bob-or-two.'

Warily, Peter felt his way in. The other, with lowered

gaze, only hunted the ground about him, as if he had lost something.

' 'Ow about it if I've catched something myself?'

'What is it?' In a vehement whisper, the bird-catcher spat his contempt. 'Sparrers?'

'Garn, not sparrers.'

'Bullfinches?'

'Better'n that.'

'What you got?'

'I ain't telling, not yet.'

'Whatcher want?'

'I ain't eaten since yesterday.'

The bird-catcher twisted his head and seemed to stare past him and through him.

'If it ain't bullfinches, what is it?'

'I'll 'elp you push your barrer, mister, for some vittels.'

'What have you catched that's better'n bullfinches? You ain't stolen nothing, 'ave you?'

'I ain't stolen anything. It's mine.'

'Suppose I got something for you to eat?' From under the broad-brimmed hat, the man briefly turned up his face and leered. 'Will you tell then?'

'What you got?'

'Some bread, maybe a bit of cheese. What you got?'

Peter gulped.

'It's a salmon.'

'You said you ain't stolen nothing.'

'Pa and me caught it in the river.'

The bird-catcher expelled a hiss of disbelief.

'Honest we did. Peg Weekes says there ain't no salmon in the Thames no more; but Pa was right. We netted 'im on the turn of the tide. He's lovely.'

'Where is he?'

'I ain't tellin' nobody until you give me that bread-and-cheese.'

'If you're telling the truth I'll give you a cock linnet of your very own. How big is he?'

'He's too big to carry. But if we get 'im into Greenwich on your barrer, we'll get a sovereign a pound for 'im. Pa said so. I'll give you summat if you'll help.'

'Who's Pa?' said the bird-catcher sibilantly.

'He's drownded.'

The information was given, and received, as if the matter wasn't worth discussion.

'I'm starving, guv. Can't you give me that bread-and-cheese?'

'Perhaps I will. I've taken a sort of liking to you. You can eat your bread-and-cheese, maybe I can find some milk too, and then we'll see your salmon, wherever you found it, and how.'

From a basket swinging on one of the handles of the barrow, the bird-catcher gave the boy a hunk of bread and a slice of cheese. With a twisted smile, he offered him milk in an oval-shaped zinc can with a brass label on the top. Then he filled a clay pipe with a broken stem and smoked it in silence as Peter ravenously filled his empty belly.

The bird-catcher was in no hurry. Morning after morning, from early dawn, he was accustomed to lying in wait for hours on end until a good catch had assembled about the call-bird under his collapsible net. He knew when to pull the string. And he was satisfied that the boy had something worth waiting for.

A salmon was money. A salmon too big for the boy to lift was worth more money than any catch of birds he had

ever made. Sixteen shillings was his best day's profit in his
life, except once, when he got the nest and eggs of a gold-
crested wren which some toff paid him a sovereign for.
Mostly he was lucky to make a shilling or two out of a
day's work: and, often enough, when the birds were shy
and he only caught hens which didn't sing, he got nothing
at all.

He barely moved when Peter wiped his mouth with the
back of his hand and, signalling him to wait, dodged into the
jungle of the marsh again. Cocking his head like a bird over
a worm he marked the boy's progress as he tunnelled
through the cover of the reeds. Then, with a sly glance up
and down the embankment, he loped in after him.

When he parted the cover over his head Peter seemed to
read his intention in his eyes. He shrank into the wet ground
as the bird-catcher, breathing heavily, searched about looking for the fish. When he spoke his voice was husky.

'Where is it?'

'I ain't tellin' you, not now.'

'Why not?'

'Because . . . that's why.'

The bird-catcher stretched out an enquiring hand and
Peter squirmed as it embraced him. His sulky protest
changed to a whine of alarm.

'Arf a mo', mister. You're not going to hurt, are you?'

The bird-catcher squeezed the scream that was on Peter's
lips into a sob. When he let him drop out of his grasp, he
was half paralysed with fear. His tormentor gazed at him,
sobbing at his feet with patches of staring skin showing
through his dishevelled rags, as disinterestedly as if he had
turned him up from underneath a stone. Hooking his foot

into the small of his back, he rolled him over. The salmon, its sleek side glittering through the covering of herbage, was exposed.

'You'll go to chokey for this,' he said. 'You pinched it off one of the boats coming up from the Medway, didn't you?'

'I didn't. I didn't. I caught it same as I said I did.'

'Ain't you had enough yet?'

He snatched at Peter's arm and twisted it behind his back.

'Do you still say you catched it?'

'Not if you'll stop touching me, I won't. Stop hurting me, mister.'

Reluctantly the bird-catcher released him. Vaguely rolling from side to side, seeming to be looking nowhere in particular, he hissed under his breath like an ostler over a horse. With eyes that seemed to have opened wider in his pale face, Peter watched him warily.

'If I stop hurting you,' the man said at last, 'and I don't tell the Johnnies, you'll be all right, won't you?'

Every shade of emotion had drained out of his voice. He might have been talking in his sleep.

'I 'aven't hurt you at all yet, not the way I could hurt you. But, if I have the salmon, I'll let you be.'

'You're not going to take it away from me?'

'Who's going to stop me?'

He thrust his face, sour with drying sweat, close to Peter's and tailed the fish in his fist. It was heavier than he had anticipated and he had to seize it in both hands to lift it. In his anguish, Peter bit his lip. The taste of blood was in his mouth. His face contorted with rage.

He sprang and, in the violence of the attack, the bird-catcher lost his balance and slipped. For a moment or two, he struggled with the fury that had closed with him, nails tearing ruts in his face and teeth sunk deep in his arm. But it couldn't last. Recovering himself, he threw Peter off as if he were dealing with a snarling cat. Like a cat, Peter rolled to his feet. Breaking through the reeds, panting for breath, he made as fast as he could for the embankment.

The call-bird on the catcher's barrow welcomed him with its tremulous pipe. Eyes misted with anger, hardly knowing what he was about, he turned on the barrow. With a sweep of his arm, he tumbled the fluttering hampers on to the footpath. Rolling the barrow on its side he kicked it hysterically with his bare feet.

Some of the hampers burst as they bounced on the ground. He wrenched out the sticks that held down the lids of the others. He kicked in the wire of the call-bird's cage, chasing it like a tin-can up the footpath.

Most of the birds flew off. The rest, those which hadn't died in the hampers, lay about, dazed and stunned, with drooping wings and ruffled plumage. The call-bird piped madly from a perch in a near-by bush.

In his fury, Peter was unaware that he was no longer alone, thoughtless of what had happened to his tormentor. But it was the bird-catcher's turn to hide.

A docker from one of the wharves up-river had strolled down the embankment. With fingers dug into his brass-studded leather belt, he watched Peter wearing himself out on the barrow with an amused grin on his weather-licked face. He was a big man, with a gold ring on one of his ears, and he affected the tight-seated moleskin trousers worn by the navvies, with 'yorks' strapped under his knees. His coat was a full-skirted jacket unbuttoned at the front and he wore a flat cap on the back of his balding head.

'Enjoying yourself?'

At the sound of his voice, which had a pleasant drainy gurgle about it, the madness that possessed Peter seeped out of him as suddenly as it had been aroused. Sheepishly, he became still and silent.

'Well, m'young cock sparrer, what's the matter?'

'He was hurting me, guv.'

'Who was?'

'Chap what's got this barrer.'

'So that's why you're bashing it about. Nice lot of linnets he had, too. Where is he now?'

'Dunno, guv. You won't let him catch me, will you?'

Peter, with a plaintive upward glance, drew closer to the big man. He gave him a friendly twist of the ear.

'It's all right, son. I know kids. What did he do to you?'

Peter dropped his head.

'Ain't telling.'

'What are you doing down here, anyhow? Skylarkin'?'

'Me and my Pa was out with the net.'

'Netting for what?'

'Salmon, guv.'

'Salmon in the river?'

'We caught one. You've gotta believe me, guv. We caught one. He's a beauty, a real whopper.'

'Garn!'

The docker raised his elbow and playfully waved it in Peter's face.

'You mean you boned it.'

'I didn't bone it. Me and Pa got it in the net off Dead Man's Point. Just out there in the run.'

'Then where's your Pa?'

'He's drownded. We lost the net and the Peelers took

the old boat. Then this chap came along and stole the fish.'

'Look 'ere, youngster. I dunno what the game is but I'm not swallowing that story. And you better mind who else you tell it to. It'll get you into trouble as sure as the Great Ship. Now 'op it.'

'You ain't going to leave me, guv. I'm afraid of him.'

Peter pulled at the docker's sleeve.

'That chap with the barrer what's been interferin' with you, eh? Where is he now?'

Peter pointed into the marsh.

'He's there somewhere.'

'All right. I'll walk up the footpath with you till you get to the 'ouses.'

'But he's got m'salmon, guv.'

'I don't care what he's got. You're better without it. You'll only have the Peelers arter you. Come on.'

Taking Peter's arm in a beefy grip, he led him, dragging like a fish on a line, along the embankment. But, after a little way, Peter gave up the struggle. Momentarily past protest he trotted obediently at the side of the amiable docker.

Half-way to Greenwich, the embankment was enlivened for a short distance by a wharf, a landing-place for cargo, with railway-sidings, trucks, and sheds. At the sight of all the activity, Peter perked up.

'Can I go now, mister?'

'Where you going?'

'Into town.'

'Got anywhere to go to?'

'Maybe.'

'You're a funny little nipper, aren't you? Look 'ere,

here's tuppence for yer. You don't deserve it, but I've sort of taken a liking to you.'

The big man extracted two coppers from a leather purse. Peter took the money eagerly and then, not believing his luck, ducked out of reach of the docker's arm. The big fellow laughed.

'All right, get along with you. And, in future, you keep off that footpath or, next time, I'll give you what for.'

Clutching the coppers, with only a brief backward glance at the man who had helped him, Peter sidled away. When he was out of sight of him, he broke into a run.

Beyond the wharf, the embankment was deserted again until it reached the cable manufactory and an engineering works on the outskirts of the town of Greenwich itself. Peter hurried on towards the wooden houses, the narrow streets, the steamer pier, the smelly decay of the waterfront where he belonged. In the crowded streets he could hold his own. Besides, he had tuppence.

When the first tumbledown houses came into view, he dragged his feet as a new purpose shaped in his mind. He tossed a passing pieman with one of his pennies; and won. Good-humouredly the pieman put down his can and, when Peter had retrieved his penny from the pavement, handed over a hot meat-filled pasty.

The pieman went on his way crying, 'Pies all 'ot! Eel, beef or mutton pies! Penny pies—all 'ot!' until his sing-song voice was lost in the distance. Wiping the crumbs off his lips, Peter wandered into an alleyway between two riverside tenements. Leaning against the wooden boards, he kept watch on the main highway.

Greenwich had the peculiarity that it was longitudinal in shape inasmuch as only one road traversed it from east to west. Anybody coming along the footpath from Charlton and Woolwich had to pass that way. Peter was waiting for the bird-catcher. It didn't matter how long he had to wait.

There was little traffic on the outskirts of the town. The clip-clop on the cobbles of a passing horse was a rarity. There were only a few street hawkers and no shops. Lurking in the shadowy slit between the tenements, Peter heard the creaking of the bird-catcher's barrow on the road before he saw him. He passed by in his greasy white smock and tall sugar-loaf hat with its floppy brim, padding in bare feet through the muck that littered the highway. The empty hampers were piled higgledy-piggledy on top of the barrow. Just in front of the handles, laid across the frame, was a hump of something carefully wrapped in a piece of wet sacking.

Slipping out of his hiding-place, keeping a safe distance, Peter followed him up the road into the town.

In East-street, he lost him among the bobbing heads of pot-hatted men and crinolined shoppers, the passing carriages, the hawkers and the barrow men shouting their wares on the pavement's edge. He jostled and pushed and puzzled a way for himself by ducking under the pole barriers put up by the navvies trenching the road for the new sewers. But the bird-catcher had vanished.

Disconsolately dragging his feet again, he zigzagged from one side of the street to the other. Then, wearily, he sat down for a while on a doorstep. He was half dozing when, out of the corner of his eye, he spotted the bird-catcher again. He was rattling the barrow, at a half-run, into a side street. But, this time, Peter didn't attempt to follow him. The wet bundle was no longer there.

Instead, when he had watched him out of sight, he made

in the direction that the bird-catcher had come from. He didn't have to search long. Outside a fishmonger's, he saw the salmon, laid in the centre of the marble slab, with a new price label stuck in its shoulder. It was the only one in the shop. At a glance, he knew it was his.

Drawing back from the shoppers discussing their purchases with the fishmonger's assistants in their blue and white striped aprons, he watched.

He was bursting to get his hands on the fish. He stared at it with bright eyes until he knew every scale on its back. Then he was filled with resentment as one of the men in the shop took the fish by the tail and drew it towards the edge of the slab. He displayed it to a customer. Drawing a long knife from his belt, he cut the great fish into two pieces. It was as if the knife had been plunged into Peter himself.

Taking the tailpiece, the fishmonger carried it away, the buyer following, to clean it. For a few moments, the outside of the shop was untenanted.

Stealing to the slab, Peter snatched at the remaining half. Gathering it under his rags, he ran, as he had never run before, away down the crowded street.

IV

STOP THIEF!

HUGGING the remains of the fish to his stomach, his bare
feet twinkling over the cobbles, Peter jinked through a
labyrinth of peg-topped trouser legs and wire-hooped
crinolines. Stumbling over the baskets of the street traders,
twisting and turning like a coursed hare among the spokes
of the carriage wheels and the hooves of the horses, he
dodged the crossing-sweepers' brooms, steered clear of
feet stuck out to trip him by boys on the costermongers'
barrows, and shied at the passengers peering down on him
from the tops of Nelsons, the local line of knife-board buses.

Nobody tried very hard to stop him. The fishmonger,
reluctant to leave the front of the shop unattended a second
time, wouldn't be drawn from the marble slab in front of
his establishment. He contented himself by waving his arms
and shouting at the fleeing figure. Someone took up the cry
of 'Stop thief!' But it was beneath the dignity of the middle-
class shoppers, in their best bibs and tuckers, to take a hand.
The draymen tickled him playfully with their whips, the
costers raised their elbows in mock threat; but they also, in
the illiterate brotherhood of the streets, had no serious
intention of interfering on the law's behalf.

When, at last, a constable appeared, red-faced and aimless,
trotting on the trail in his long-skirted coat, wide belt, and

pot-hat, he was given an ironic cheer. By that time, Peter had no need to run.

He had reached the sanctuary of dark alleys, drunken stairways, earthy smells and secret places. To the middle-class families who lived in the rows of good houses leading up to and fringing the Park and Blackheath; to the respectable folk who came to see the Observatory, with its time-staff and ball, the Painted Hall with its relics of Nelson, and the Parish Church with its memories of General Wolfe, the conqueror of Canada; to the people to whom cleanliness was next to godliness, the Greenwich of the waterfront was a left-over, as Pa Smelley had been, of a less enlightened age. It belonged to the time before the old town had lost its maritime importance; before the trains, the paddle-steamers and the newfangled water-closets had sounded, each with their own particular music, the wonders of human progress.

People didn't care to be reminded of it; but the rich stinks, the rotting wharves and the rickety tenements of the waterfront were the real Greenwich. Most of the town's population dwelt there.

To Peter, the network of wooden buildings laid so close together that you could jump from rooftop to rooftop across the alleyways dividing them, the wooden wharves, the stairs down to the Thames, the mouldering decay, was home.

Among the refuse that littered the cobbles he found a piece of sailcloth. Laying it out he wrapped the head and shoulders of the fish inside it. Then, tucking the damp bundle under his arm, holding it with both hands, he made his way to a narrow passage, no wider than a door, which passed through the middle of one of the buildings.

The passage led to a court about fifty yards long and three yards wide. Enclosing it were lofty wooden houses,

some of them six storeys high with abutments in the upper
floors which bulged and leaned towards each other, block-
ing out the light. Scraps of washing dangled overhead. At
the windows mob-capped hussies with uncombed hair, many
of them with infants at their breasts, gossiped shrilly across
the gap. The courtyard itself seethed with a crowd of
loungers and children, mostly children.

The tenement, where whole families were housed in
single rooms sharing cooking facilities in a communal
kitchen, was named, improbably, Palace Buildings. An attic
in it, at the top of six flights of trembling stairs, was where
Peter had belonged with Pa ever since he could remember.

Ordinarily, he regarded the yard with its quarrelsome
gang of his own kind as his private stamping-ground. He
had no particular friends because boys of his age seldom
have. But, in the give-and-take of the Buildings, he could
hold his own; and he enjoyed it.

For once, he wished that the yard was empty; that he
could dispose the precious package without the other boys
wanting to know what he had got. He hesitated; and the
others sensed it. One of the urchins, seeing him appear,
stuck his thumbs in his ears and spreading his fingers danced
about him chanting, 'Georgie Porgy puddeny-pie.' Peter
tried to pass him.

The incident caught the attention of a group. Bored with
a game of hopscotch, they formed a half-circle barring his
path and parroted a nonsense song.

> *'Ena mina mic-mac*
> *Tick-tack tick-tack*
> *Ooza booza back-a-bay*
> *Ah-var vis . . .'*

Red-faced, Peter tried to push through them. The children only crowded in on him the more.

'What you got there?'

'Never mind what I got.'

'He's boned it.'

'I 'aven't. It's mine.'

'What you got?'

'I ain't tellin'.'

'If you don't tell, I'll bash you.'

The rest kept up the infuriating gibberish:

> *'Jamsetjee ma jabajehoy*
> *Jabbery do bi porie*
> *Ikey Pikey, Sikey, Crikey*
> *Chillungow ullabadorie.'*

When they had finished they started again. By now most of the children in the yard had joined in. Clinging to the bundle, baffled and helpless, Peter sniffed.

'Cry baby!'

One of the bigger boys made a grab. Another, making the most of an advantage, pushed him from behind. He stumbled under the pressure and, as he went down on his knees, he lost his hold on the fish. It was picked up by an urchin who, holding it high over his head in its wrapping of sailcloth, jigged with derision.

Crouched on the ground, Peter rose on his toes for a spring. The other boys, with the satisfaction of people who have precipitated an issue in which they are unwilling to get involved themselves, drew back to watch the outcome.

'Bash him, Peter.'

'I'm on your side, mate.'

'Give 'im the old one one-two.'

Peter wasn't listening. All he could think of was the salmon that, once again, had been taken from him. With a furious rush he spun the other boy off his feet. He didn't use his fists. He grappled on the ground with him for the possession of the thing, now only half the thing, which was all his own.

In the struggle, the wrapping of sailcloth burst open. The lump of salmon slithered across the yard. Spreadeagled over the boy who had snatched it from him, pommelling him with flailing arms, he couldn't reach it.

'Avast there . . . Belay . . .'

A quavering voice, sounding over the turmoil like the cry of a gull in a high wind, startled Palace Buildings into quiet. The attention of the mob of idlers and children was diverted. Peter, locked on the ground with his adversary, stiffened with surprise.

The newcomer was a quaintly-dressed figure in a square-cut blue coat with great cuffs, white cravat and three-cornered hat. Ringlets of grey hair straggled over his collar. His face was mapped with age. He had a wooden leg and he supported himself with stout sticks in each hand. Peg Weekes—everybody in the town knew him—was half crazed, he was usually half-seas over; but he was one of the last survivors of Nelson's navy. He had served as a topman in the flagship at Trafalgar and it was said that Sir Thomas Hardy himself, when he was Governor of the Hospital, had given him a berth. Like the hulks on the riverside, Peg Weekes had outlived his time long enough to have become a local landmark.

'All hands out and down . . . I'll start you, you little lubbers.'

With a vigour that made the urchins shrink, he brought down a stick on the shoulders and backs of any of them within reach. Clearing a respectful circle, he used his peg leg to limpet Peter off the belly of his opponent.

'It weren't my fault, Peg. Honest it weren't.'

'Silence between decks,' ordered Peg authoritatively. Addressing the yard generally he added: 'As for the rest of you scum, get below!'

Some of the lookers-on smirked. The women at the windows squawked in challenge. The children made grimaces. Peg leaned on his sticks, and glared.

'I said batten down your hatches . . .'

He paused to let his words take effect.

'The Johnnies is coming aboard.'

The tenants of Palace Buildings needed no second warning. There was hardly one of them with a clear conscience. The crowd in the yard, at first with an almost imperceptible movement, latterly with an ill-concealed anxiety, melted away. In the upper floors of the buildings windows were closed. Pushing his sticks into one hand Peg grabbed Peter by the arm.

'It's you, matey,' he whispered hoarsely. They're arter you.'

'Where's the fish, Peg?'

'What fish?'

'The salmon. Somebody's lifted it.'

'What you narkin' about? The Peelers is arter you. I heard 'em myself asking about you from Polly at the "Fortune of War." Peg, sez I, there's something he's been a doing of; no doubt as to that, no doubt at all.'

'I ain't done nothing wrong.'

'That's what they all sez, Peter, that's what they all sez. But they seize you up just the same. They flog your back

into raw liver, same as mine was. I'm tellin' you; I stumped
down here on m'old peg leg just to tell you. The Peelers is
arter you. I heard 'em say to Polly, plain as I'm talking to
you now, and it made m'blood run cold, boy; sez they,
when did you see him last?'

'What did Polly say?'

'Didn't wait to listen what Polly sez,' said Peg conspiratorially. 'I just sez to myself, sez I, I gotta give m'old
shipmate the wink.'

'What'll they do to me?'

'If the Peelers get you . . . why, you'll get forty lashes
at least. That's what I reckon, under Queen's Regulations.
Forty at least. Enough to make your bowels and kidneys
ache for the rest of your born days.'

With increasing agitation, Peg whispered terror into the
boy's ear. It didn't matter that the broken old man was only
reliving the savagery of his own life in the lower decks of
the navy half a century earlier. Peter believed him. Pa was
right about the salmon; he had no doubt that Peg was right
about the fate that awaited him if he was caught by the
Peelers.

'Strip for punishment, that's what they'll say. I dream
about it now, boy; the stroke that makes your face go black
and your lungs fit to burst. Then the long wait for the next
one, while they wipe the blood and skin off the tails of the
cat. And the next one that makes all the lashes before seem
as sweet as grog. Peg, sez I to myself, when I hear the
Peelers is arter you, I don't want that to happen to a fine
upstanding lad like him. So I comes to find you afore they
do.'

A lounger, who had been standing guard at the entrance
to the buildings, gave a two-fingered whistle. Dodging into

a dark hole in the warren of doorways he gave a parting shout of 'Police.'

With unexpected agility, still keeping his grip on Peter's arm, Peg hustled the boy into the gloom of a dank stairway. They sheltered there as two constables came heavily into the now-deserted yard. One of them knocked with his truncheon on one of the doorways. A tousle-haired woman, with a clutch of children pressing behind her, opened it just wide enough to put her head through the crack. The constables evidently reassured her because, after a few moments' conversation, she issued into the courtyard and pointed to an entrance at the far end. As she did so, more and more people in the Buildings, realising that they themselves were not involved, made a sulky reappearance.

The woman was directing the police to the attic which Peter had shared with Pa. As the policemen moved off to investigate, Peg breathed hotly in Peter's ear.

'What did I tell you? You gotta make a run for it.'

'I want my fish.'

'What's all this about a fish?'

'We caught one at Dead Man's Island same as Pa said we would.'

Breathlessly, Peter poured out his story.

'You believe me, don't you, Peg?'

'What I believe won't save you from a red-checked shirt at the gangplank. It's what the Peelers think, that's what matters. Take the advice of an old tar, matey. That story wouldn't put wind in the sail of a captain's gig.'

'But if I got the fish I could prove it.'

'It'll prove you pinched it, that's what it'll prove. Your Pa was balmy, boy. Maybe I'm balmy, too. But not that balmy, not ole Peg.'

'Won't nobody ever believe me?'

'Why do you think the Peelers are arter you? Why do you think I came here if it wasn't to warn you in time? You've got to jump ship, that's what you gotta do; jump ship afore they seize you up.'

'I ain't got nowhere to go.'

'You can go to sea same as I did. Stow away on one of them barges going down to Gravesend. Sign on in one of them newfangled steamers.'

'Don't want to, Peg. I'm frightened.'

'Think how you'll feel when the Peeler pulls out the cat from its red-baize bag. Did you know that, Peter? They always keep it in a red-baize bag just so the blood doesn't show when they put it away dirty . . .'

'No, Peg . . . let me go . . .'

'It's as true as I'm telling you. When they cut you down afterwards . . .'

'No . . . no . . .'

The grip of fear was more powerful than Peg's grip on his arm. Peter broke away from him and darted into the courtyard. He glanced about to make sure that the Peelers were still out of view. Then he slipped into a passage, filled with the stink of cooking and tobacco smoke, into the kitchen where the tenants of the buildings gathered to prepare their meals.

In the thick atmosphere an auction was in progress. A rag-bag of men, women and children, milled noisily over and under a narrow table, served with benches, where an individual, with the penetrating voice of a street trader, was waving a long kitchen knife in the air.

'Fip-pence? Flippin' fip-pence? Look 'ere, Ma. I'll take a

tanner and a flag. All right then, seven browns for a thin slice.'

He lowered the knife to cut off the piece. On the floor children gambled over games of knucklebones and marbles. At the naked gas jets, sticking out from the wall, men lit their pipes in the spade-shaped flame. The iron cooking-range, along one side of the kitchen, hissed and spat at women tending pots and pans.

It was difficult for the newcomer to focus immediately what was going on. Peter stood blinking at the entrance, unnoticed by the excited rabble round the table, checked by a barrier of sound, stinks, smoke and sour-smelling humanity. To a chorus of heckling and jeers, the man with the knife raised the blade over his head again.

'The werry last piece, ladies and gents, the sweetest cut from behind the eyes. Straight from the 'Gate and fresh as little Kate. I'll toss any of you six mouldies or nuffink.'

A weasel of a man took the bet. As a penny made an arc over the table, the man with the knife called, 'Heads.' The coin dropped on the floor and rolled out of sight. There was a scrimmage among the onlookers to find which had won.

In a bloody mess on the deal-table Peter sighted what was left of the salmon. It was little more than a head. The rest was already frying and boiling in communal pots on the gas range. Seizing advantage of the diversion in search of the lost penny, he crept up to the table and snatched his prize.

An empty gin bottle, thrown at him by a sozzled indivi-dual in a corner, shattered on the wall behind him. Momen-tarily, one of the children on the floor arrested him with a clutch on his leg. He kicked himself free. In the hubbub the man who had brandished the knife saw him flee down the passage into the courtyard. He half got to his feet to go after him. Then he began to laugh. He laughed until all the other thieves in the kitchen were laughing too.

Peter didn't dare to hesitate as he streaked into the yard. His adversaries were behind him as well as in front. But, as he emerged into the open, there were no Peelers waiting, and no sign of Peg Weekes either. He didn't dally to find out why.

Thrusting the fish-head into his pocket as he ran, he confused his trail by turning down every side-turning that presented itself. He knew his way in Greenwich like a mouse in its run; like a mouse, he was too small to attract attention.

The day was almost over. The lamp-lighters, with their poles on their shoulders, were starting their evening round of the streets. Naphtha flares were burning under the awnings of the coffee stalls and the shell-fish barrows. The streets were quiet because the people, who had homes to go to, had retired for tea.

When he felt free from pursuit, he slowed his pace. He even amused himself, when he found a newly-laid pavement in the modern part of the town, trying to walk over the blocks without putting his feet on the cracks. It helped to keep him warm.

After a while, he was drawn to the light of an open door which a few stragglers were entering for some sort of a meeting. He guessed it was a mission hall, and he reckoned that he might be taken in for a cup of soup or tea. Idly, he crossed the road and made a noise by kicking about a tin he found lying in the gutter.

The ruse worked. A beaming charity worker, in a black

frock-coat, appeared at the door and, in a voice as if he had a hot potato in his mouth, called Peter to him.

'Haven't you got any home to go to, my son?'

'No, guv'nor. I'm a ragged child.'

'Dear me. Do you go to the ragged school?'

'No. I ain't been learned. T'ain't my fault. 'Ave you gotta cup of tea? I ain't 'ad anything, guv'nor—honest, I 'aven't—all day.'

He put on the forlorn and imploring voice of the professional starveling.

'Yes, I think we can find you a cup of tea, and a bun. We might even be able to help in getting you into a suitable institution.'

At the dread word, Peter shrank. In his mind the word institution had come to mean the sort of restraint that he associated with ugly words like prison and reformatory and school. He wasn't far wrong. But he didn't say anything. He wanted some tea.

'If I take you into God's house, will you pray to Him?'

It was odd that all grown-ups, Pa included, were so anxious for him to pray. He didn't mind. He wanted to eat. He nodded his head vigorously.

'Then, my child, come into His arms.'

With a sweep of his own in invitation, the missioner stood back, beaming at his own benevolence, to show the way to heaven. Peter went in.

It was a bare hall with a simple altar at the far end; rows of chairs down the middle, and a trestle table at the back furnished with a tea urn, pyramids of mugs, and plates sparsely provisioned with doorsteps of currant bread, without much evidence of any currants. Under an oleograph of the Queen and her Consort, a thin-lipped, tightly-stayed woman, with a spinsterish air and a stern attitude of self-denial, was economically dispensing the refreshments to a group of people who had plainly come to the mission to eat rather than to be saved.

The missioner, with an avuncular hand resting on Peter's shoulder, shepherded him to the trestle.

'Another little fish for our big net, my dear Miss Fawdry.'

He smiled expansively.

'I fancy he needs a little material help before he can be enriched with the spiritual consolation he so clearly hungers for.'

Miss Fawdry quizzed Peter distastefully.

'He certainly looks as if he needs a good bath—with kitchen soap, too.'

'Perhaps we can persuade our good Dr Barnrooth—that is, if the funds are available—to interest himself in the case. The boy tells me that he hasn't a home to go to. But that can wait until the more important business of the service, and the magic lantern lecture. You'll enjoy that, you young ragamuffin, won't you?'

With a mouth crammed with dry bread, Peter could only nod. Miss Fawdry tossed her head at him.

'Thirty-two bites, please, for every mouthful. You won't get any more.'

The missioner looked about him with a resigned smile.

'Not a very good attendance, Miss Fawdry. Still, we must make allowance for these bleak winter evenings. Has the lecturer arrived yet? Ah, my dear sir, how much we are looking forward to your address. Were you in the Holy Land long?'

The missioner passed out of hearing in a burble of polite nothings. Peter pushed the last crust of currant bread into his mouth, washing it down with the dregs of his tea, as Miss Fawdry determinedly settled down to the duty of ushering the reluctant guests into their places. Peter slipped into a chair at the back. He didn't mind looking at magic lantern slides and, after the tea, he felt sleepy.

The service began with Miss Fawdry squeezing the notes of a hymn out of a harmonium, and the missionary, singing with slow emphasis, trying to squeeze a few sounds out of the congregation. Then, in a sing-song voice, he read the lessons; so soporifically that Peter's chin dropped on his chest. He dozed.

He was awakened by a sharp twitch of the ear. Miss Fawdry, having vacated the harmonium, had come up behind him to make sure that he enjoyed the consolations of religion in full measure.

When he awoke, the missioner had left the front of the hall to adjust the magic lantern at the back. The lamp inside was smoking furiously, filling the hall with fumes which were as much a preamble to a magic lantern lecture as the tuning-up of the orchestra before the overture of a grand opera. In front of the altar, a sheet had been strung up; and the lecturer was waiting to begin.

'I fancy we may have the lights lowered now, Miss Fawdry.'

When the taps of the gas jets had been turned down to a flicker, and the contretemps of a first slide turned upside down had been corrected, the address began; punctuated by a clicking device used by the lecturer to indicate when he required the next picture to be moved on.

Peter liked the coloured slides, especially of the fishermen in the sea of Galiliee and the Roman soldiers in their armour. He couldn't understand why people wore the funny clothes they did or why the Holy Land was more holy than Greenwich. There didn't seem much to choose between the way people behaved in either place. But he had come to the conclusion that religion was unpredictable. It was just something, like praying, you had to accept to please people who boxed your ears if you didn't.

Towards the end of the lecture something went wrong. The lecturer and the missioner, and Miss Fawdry, had to check the remaining slides to search for one which seemed to be unaccountably missing. The audience coughed and shuffled about in their seats. Peter suddenly recollected what the missioner had said about sending him to an institution.

While the lights were still lowered, he slipped quietly out of his chair. Keeping a wary eye on Miss Fawdry, he backed towards the door.

No wonder they called it a magic lantern. As he stepped back into the streets the real world mocked the coloured slides. While the lecturer drooled on, the fog had drifted down. Greenwich was swathed in monotone; a grey shroud that muffled the gaslight, a sheet that deadened sound and divided those who were out and about one from another.

Peter almost walked into a policeman. Just in time he spotted the lantern slotted in the Peeler's belt. He made the best of his luck by lifting an apple off a barrow as he walked past. In East-street, where they were building the sewers, he shared the charcoal brazier of a night-watchman.

He accepted his situation as he found it. He had been just a little less than homeless all his life. It was only when he began to feel hungry again that he slipped furtively and familiarly through the fog to a public house whose lights glowed wanly through frosted glass windows.

It was known as the 'Fortune of War.' It took its name from an inn-sign showing a jovial pensioner, who had lost both legs and an arm in the wars, raising a foaming tankard of ale with his remaining limb. Inside, the customers were singing a hoarse chorus to the music of a concertina.

When he had made sure that he was unobserved, Peter bent down to find the iron ring in the flaps opening into the cellar below. With the ease of long practice, he swung open the trap-door and dropped on to the chute which the brewer's men used to lower in the barrels of beer. He hung on just long enough to lower the trap quietly on top of him. Then, letting go, he slid into the sour-smelling cellar underneath.

A low gas jet illuminated the scene. Feeling his way among the rows of barrels, he climbed a wooden ladder to another trap-door in the roof. After listening for a while to the clamour in the bar, he knocked three times with his fist on the woodwork. When there was no response, he climbed two steps higher on the ladder and, bending his head, raised the trap-door a few inches on his shoulders. With his hands gripping the brink, he peered hopefully along the floor behind the bar.

He could see Polly's crinoline flaunting behind her as she leant over to talk to a customer. He could sniff tobacco smoke and stale beer, and hear the familiar chatter of the regulars. Temporarily, they had stopped singing.

He waited until the concertina wheezed into action again and Polly moved towards the beer taps to fill another mug. Cautiously stretching an arm, the fugitive tugged the end of her skirt.

'Polly!'

V

THE 'FORTUNE OF WAR'

POLLY didn't so much as glance down. She steadily drew the porcelain beer-tap to its limit and, while her head was lowered to top up the tankard, talked out of the corner of her mouth.

'So there's the bad penny. Where you been? They're looking for you.'

'Peg told me they was.'

'I said they'd find you in the Buildings. Ain't you been there?'

'I skipped. I was afeared, Pol.'

'Afeared of what?'

'The Peelers.'

'Stuff and nonsense.'

With a swish of her skirt she moved off with the beer. Someone on the other side of the bar chi-iked her as she passed. With a toss of her head she set down the pot on the mahogany counter and collected the coppers.

To the accompaniment of the concertina, one of the customers was rendering a solo. With fervent expression he intoned:

'On the other side of Jordon, in the sweet fields of Eden
Where the Tree of Life is blooming, there is rest for you.'

Apparently unmoved by the sentiment, Polly dispensed drinks and kept up a cheerful exchange of back-chat with the people lounging on the brass rail.

'No, there isn't room for a gin in that pint. And, young man, I'll ask you kindly to keep your hands off me. A small port, dear, for a big girl like you . . .'

The barmaid at the 'Fortune of War' was popular; and deservedly so. She had a dimple which invited a chuck under the chin; and she wasn't averse to permitting favoured customers to take the liberty. When she leant over the bar to mop up the beer stains, she offered a glimpse of two full white breasts. When she turned to pick up a bottle from the ornate overmantel of mahogany and glass behind her, she swung the great bell of her crinoline with provocative grace. She was a hussy; but she was a self-reliant and warm-hearted one.

'Pol!'

Tired of waiting, Peter called again, through the crack in the trap-door.

'Can't you see I'm busy?'

'I'm hungry.'

From the debris under the counter she picked out the remains of a meat pie, which somebody hadn't finished, and dropped it within reach of his arm. He stretched out for it eagerly.

'Peg sez, if the Peelers get me, they'll flog me same as they flogged him.'

'Garn, you don't believe what Peg tells you.'

'But the Peelers is arter me, ain't they?'

'Course they are. They've found your old Pa.'

'I couldn't help it, Pol: I couldn't even hold the net.'

'Nobody says you could. One of the bargees hooked him

out at Bugsby's. They've been dragging the reach for you, too. Thought you'd both been drownded. Him and his netting. I said it'd end in trouble.'

'We caught a fish, Pol.'

'Must 'ave been a long time dead.'

'He wasn't. I got his head in m'pocket.'

Polly sniffed.

'Like the time when you said you'd got a tanner for steak-and-kidney pud, when you hadn't.'

The customers in the 'Fortune of War' were starting to drift away. There were no more choruses. One by one, with calls of 'Good night, Pol,' they stepped into the fog. Polly settled herself on a stool and, kicking off her shoes, rested while she could. Normally she was on her feet from seven in the morning until the small hours of the next.

'I ain't lying this time, Pol,' said the small voice beside her. 'If you'll come into the cellar I'll show him to you.'

'To see an old fish head? Get away with you.'

She yawned. In the misery of poverty and sweated labour, life was only bearable if you didn't think about it too much. Polly herself had little enough to be grateful for. Her home was an iron bedstead and a few sticks of furniture in the roof of the pub. She worked seven days a week; and the only occasion when she had had time off in her life was when she was far gone in an illegitimate pregnancy. She never saw the father again. Grim necessity had forced her to leave the infant on a doorstep. It was Peter that, subsequently, she suckled at her breast.

She was almost dozing when a newcomer came into the bar parlour, hastily shutting out the fog behind him.

'Coo, what a night. Out there you can 'ardly see your hand in front of yer.'

Polly sat up welcomingly.

'Why, hello stranger!'

'Hello, Pol.'

She stepped into her shoes and, starting to her feet, gave herself away by stealing a glance over her shoulder at the mirror and making a dab at her hair.

'I vow she's looking more handsome than ever.'

'Get away with you, Mr 'Opkins. Why, you haven't been to see me for ages. What brings you to town on a night like this?'

'I've had a bit o' luck, Pol. M'old mum's passed over—remember, her what had the whelk stall by the 'Trafalgar'—and, bless her old heart, she's left a few jimmy o'goblins for me. So, what with the fog, and a little of what you fancy jingling in m'pocket, I thought I'd pop in to see m'old Dutch again. What'll you'ave, m'lady? Mine's a milk stout.'

Polly bobbed a mocking curtsy. With a 'Thank you, kind sir,' she said she would like a glass of port. Soon the two of them put their heads together over the counter in the intimacy of old flames.

Peter raised the hatch in the floor a little higher to listen. From the moment the new customer came in his voice had sounded familiar. It was deep, with a drainy gurgle in it; the sort of voice you couldn't easily forget. When he heard its owner telling Pol that he was working at Angerstein's, he knew for sure that it was the docker who had got him away from the bird-catcher and given him tuppence at the wharf for himself.

'I thought I said you wasn't to come behind the bar.'

As Peter emerged through the trap-door, Polly caught hold of him by his ear.

'You go back where you belong, or go into the scullery and get some of that dirt off you. My, you're filthy.'

'Arf a mo, Pol,' interrupted the docker. 'I've seen you before, ain't I?'

'Yes, mister.'

Eagerly, Peter dived his hand into his pocket and, producing the fish-head, held it up for inspection.

'There you are. I told you Pa and me had caught a salmon. That's 'is 'ead.'

'What happened to the rest of him?' the docker enquired humorously. 'Eaten it?'

'They pinched it off me; the bird-catcher and them people at the Buildings.'

The docker and Polly exchanged looks. She released her hold on his ear.

'That's the same story he told me this morning when I found him breaking up one of them bird-catcher's barrers. Might be, Pol?'

She stared at him doubtfully.

'He doesn't often tell the truth.'

Peter waved the remains of the salmon.

'That's 'is 'ead to prove it.'

'Yes, you've got a fish's head all right,' said the docker. 'But how's Pol and me to know you didn't pinch it?'

The big fellow's weathered face was wrinkled in interrogation. Pulling at his belt, he was trying to make up his mind whether he ought to take it off and give the boy a licking; or take him at his word.

He was still indecisive when the door of the pub was pushed open again. A Peeler appeared out of the murk, pausing for another one who was close behind him. With a nod, Polly indicated the new arrivals to the docker. He made a half-turn of interest. Filled with panic, Peter ranged about for a line of escape. Before the Peelers were through the door, he ducked under the counter and, lifting the wire hoop of Polly's crinoline, slipped underneath it.

He wrapped an arm round the pear-shape of her leg. Buried in her petticoats he murmured a faint agitated appeal.

'You won't split on me, Pol. Promise you won't give me up.'

In her surprise she stood quite still. Then she put out a hand, as if she was smoothing her dress, and pressed down through the balloon of stuff to give him a comforting pat. The docker, when he noticed that Peter had vanished, was on the point of exclaiming. She checked him with a warning shake of her head.

The Peelers brought with them a smell of fog and lamp-oil. The fog had seeped into their uniforms; the fumes rose from the crimped chimneys of the lanterns in their belts. In spite of the weather, they were a cheerful red-faced couple with generous whiskers, who made no bones that they were glad of the excuse to come inside in the course of duty. As a gesture of friendliness, they lifted off their pot-hats, and planted them on the counter.

'Any luck?' Polly enquired.

'No, looks as if he's a drowner, too. He ain't been back to the room in Palace Buildings. Peg Weekes says he hasn't seen him, and he hasn't been 'ere. Never mind; by all accounts, he won't be much of a loss to the world. What about a pint for two thirsty coppers?'

'Is it on the house?'

'That's up to you, ducks.'

As she turned to take the beer mugs off the hook, Peter moved with her like a monkey on a pole. The warmth of his skinny frame pressing into the soft flesh of her leg aroused in her a feeling which had been suppressed since the time when she fed him at her breast. Suddenly, she didn't want to give him up. She had given up too much already. He was a substitute for the child she had had to abandon of her own.

The unexpected presence of Bert Hopkins had had a softening effect on her, too. Of all the men in her life, he had been at once the gentlest and the strongest. He had never knocked her about, as most of the others did, and he was the one who, in the end, always came back to her. When she had drawn the beer for the policemen, she filled another loving pot for him.

While she worked the beer pumps, Peter crouched on the floor. When she got up, he again hung tensely on her legs, both his arms wrapped about her thighs.

'Here's health, ducks,' said one of the Peelers, 'and here's hoping for an easier beat tomorrer.'

'What'll you do if the boy turns up?'

'Well, he'll have to tell us what happened and, once we've established his identity, he can collect the boat and the net, what's left of it. One of them paddle-steamers cut it up. Not that a net's going to be any use to him. Didn't do Pa Smelley much good.'

'He's not in trouble then,' said Polly.

'Not as far as we know. Has 'e been in trouble before?'

'Not more than other boys.'

The other Peeler joined in.

'I'm sick of boys today. While we've been looking for this one, a bird-catcher comes into the station with a story about a mudlark breaking up his barrow . . .'

Peter pressed more tightly on Polly's legs.

'Then we had another one reported this morning for snatching a lump of fish off the slab at Cheap's.'

'What sort of fish?' asked the docker.

'Don't rightly know. One of our chaps said it was a salmon. You don't often see 'em about nowadays, do you?'

Polly and the docker stared at each other. She could feel Peter trembling. The policemen interpreted the uncomfortable silence as a signal that it was time to move. They smacked their lips and stroked the foam out of their moustaches.

'Well, I expect you're wanting to put the shutters up. We shall be making another routine call tomorrow, Miss. If the kid shows up, we shall be obliged if you keep your hands on him. If he doesn't, and we find him in the river, we'll notify you. This fog don't make nothing any easier. Well, so long.'

The Peelers picked up their hats.

'Good night, Miss.'

'Good night, constable. Good night.'

Polly and the docker watched them out of the door. Then she reached for the hem of her skirt. With a sweep she lifted one side of the hoop high over her head.

'They've gone,' she said expressionlessly.

The docker gravely unhooked his belt. Peter didn't move. His face was buried in her generous flank and, in his terror, he dug his nails into her skin.

'I told you he was a liar.'

With the wing of her crinoline still held over her head, she stared emptily ahead of her. She knew that she oughtn't to have been surprised but, however briefly, she had yielded to an emotion that had filled her with a strange happiness.

Momentarily the hardness had gone; she was soft, through and through. But it had ended . . . the way it always ended.

'I'll deal with him.'

Bert Hopkins stretched over the counter and put out a hand to seize the shrinking figure. With an evasive wriggle, Peter froze on to her again. She felt angry, and ashamed. It was to hide from herself that she dropped her skirt over the top of him again.

'No, Bert, don't thrash 'im. He isn't worth it.'

Her voice was resigned, but there was a menacing edge to it.

'What are you going to do about him?'

'I don't know. I tell you I don't know.'

The dam of her emotions broke. With sudden abandon, shrilling hysterically, she struggled to free herself from the thing—he didn't seem like flesh and blood any more—limpeted to her body.

'Go away, you little bastard. Let go of me, I say. Let go.'

Clawing under her skirt, she freed one of his arms but, when she reached for the other, he desperately locked himself about her again. His dead weight, hobbling her legs, made her reel. Losing balance, she sat down heavily in the sawdust with her crinoline gaping over her like an upturned tent.

As her legs flew up in the fall, Peter rolled on to her and twisted his own round her calves. He had no thought as to why he was doing it. In his terror he had ceased to have a separate existence; all he knew was that he must never be prised from Polly's warm body again. Sweating with the exertion, breathing heavily, the two of them remained locked on the ground.

Bert Hopkins lifted the flap of the bar counter and slipped

the latch in the gate underneath. The flash of Polly's white legs flailing the air, the heat of her emotion, had disturbed him, too, with a sense of physical awareness. Her mouth was parted, her eyes were melting and her hair was in dis-array. She had almost stopped struggling. She lay back while Peter, tensed in every limb, clung like a bat to its mother.

Leaning over the two of them, the docker put a big hand round Peter's waist to lift him off. But the boy's arms and legs held like steel bands. He caught him by the scruff of his coat. Peter swung his head and buried his teeth savagely in his arm.

With an oath Bert Hopkins dragged him clear, and spiralled him through the wicket gate in the counter into the parlour beyond.

'Now get out!'

'Won't.'

'Do you want a larruping as well?'

As Polly climbed wearily to her feet, Peter pulled out the battered fish-head. In a gesture of defiance he hurled it at his adversary. It was a good aim. It hit Bert Hopkins on the side of the head and slithered off to fall behind the bar. Sticking out his tongue, Peter turned and, without waiting for the consequences, made for the door. He took one backward glance as the fog swirled in to embrace him. Then he was gone.

The docker walked up behind her as she lazily tidied her-self in the mirror.

'Are you all right, Pol? he asked gently.

'Yes, I'm all right. What do you think'll happen to him?'

'Do you care?'

She shrugged hopelessly. Bert Hopkins put his hands on her shoulders.

'Give us a kiss, Pol?'

'Can't you see I don't want that?'

'Why not?'

'Because . . .'

He tried to turn her towards him.

'I love you.'

'That's what they all say. Take your hands away. Can't yer see I don't want to be touched? Not now.'

'I thought you liked me.'

'If you liked me, you'd know to leave me alone. Haven't I been messed about with enough already?'

'You've let that mudlark upset you. You don't want to worry about him. Come on, let's kiss and forget.'

In his ardour, he twisted her round and forced his lips on to hers. She clenched her teeth and closed her eyes resentfully.

'Come on, Pol, be a sport.'

He pressed her back towards a cubby-hole at the back of the bar.

She yielded coldly, resentfully.

Couldn't he understand that a woman didn't want a man like this? Didn't he know that there was a rhythm of things that you couldn't turn up and down like a gas tap? But none of them did. They just wanted what they wanted when they wanted it. That was love.

'Thanks, Pol.'

Unemotionally, she rearranged her ruffled dress a second time. Avoiding his eyes, she filled half a tumbler with spirit and took a choking gulp. Bert Hopkins' features were wrinkled in bewilderment.

'Wasn't it all right?'

'Of course it wasn't. Won't nobody ever understand?'

'But you like me, don't you?'

'You know I do, Bert. Come on, ducks, it's time I shut the pub and you went home.'

He still lingered on while she busied her hands washing and polishing glasses, trying to drive out from her mind the dull ache of frustration and loss. Wrapped in their own reflections neither of them noticed the bare-footed entry of the man in a grimy white smock and a tall-crowned floppy-brimmed black hat.

It was the bird-catcher, drunk. With a faint smile he weaved his way to the bar, attracting attention by tapping the wood with a milled edge of a coin. Polly measured him up across the counter.

'What do you want?'

Rolling his head, the bird-catcher continued to smile stupidly.

'If you want a drink, you'll have to hurry. I'm putting the shutters up. Looks as if you're broached-to already. All right, what is it?'

With a hiccup that was itself a whisper he asked for porter. While Polly went to fill the pot he placed the coin on the counter. She swept it up, without looking, in the same movement that she set down the beer. She didn't realise what it was until she had it in her hand.

Opening her palm, she stared unbelievingly at the fat silver piece, struck on the obverse with the head of the young Queen Victoria and, on the reverse, with the shield of the Royal Arms. It was a five-shilling bit. To her it could mean only one thing. The superstition was widespread that any barmaid who accepted one was doomed to lose her job, or worse.

'What's the matter, Pol.'

In answer to Bert Hopkins' quiet enquiry, she leant forward and dashed the mug out of the bird-catcher's hand. The beer doused him as the pewter pot clattered on to the floor. With a pale face Polly handed back the coin.

'You know I can't take that.'

'It's all I got left.'

Swaying on his feet, averting his head, he looked slyly about him. Slopped with beer, filled up to the neck with it, he was an object to stir disgust even in the gutters of Victorian London. Bert Hopkins advanced on him questioningly.

'I want to ask you summat. How did you come by that five-shilling bit in the first place? You didn't get it honest: I know you didn't.'

Evading his gaze, with darting glances at the floor in front and behind the counter, the bird-catcher spotted the bruised fish-head in the sawdust.

'Where did you get that?' he said softly. 'Was it Cheap's the fishmongers?'

'What are you at?'

'I only asked.'

'What's that go to do with the five-shilling piece?'

The bird-catcher lolled his head, and smiled remotely.

'Come on, out with it.'

'There ain't much salmon in Greenwich, mister. That's the one I sold to Cheap's this morning. You can ask 'em if you like.'

Bert Hopkins looked at him hard.

'Did you hear him, Pol?'

'Why can't we get rid of him?' she said. 'I'm tired.'

'You·'aven't been listening.'

Bert Hopkins was a slow thinker. It took him a perceptible

time to organise the suspicion that was shaping in his mind. The bird-catcher sensed his mood. He stepped back a dizzy pace or two as a sudden fear penetrated his stupor. The docker, his mind made up, moved after him and twisted his big fist into the yoke of the smock.

' 'Ere?'

'What's the game? I ain't done you no harm.'

The bird-catcher, with a pleading whine, shrank underneath him until he was almost on his knees. The docker was grim.

'Are you a bird-catcher?' He shook him. 'Are you?'

'Ain't no crime in that.'

'You had your barrer turned over by a kid down-river this morning. You told the Peelers about it.'

'It was a good catch, mister. I'm a poor man.'

'And you made another catch, too, didn't you? You took that salmon off the kid what you sold to Cheap's.'

' 'E'd pinched it.'

'You dirty liar.'

Lifting him by his smock, the docker raised his other fist and hit the bird-catcher full in the mouth. The blow sent him spinning against the wall. When his head touched, he dropped in an untidy heap on the floor. Blowing on his clenched fist, Bert Hopkins turned to Polly.

She seemed unaware of her surroundings. With glazed eyes, she stood stiffly behind the bar, behaving as if she was on the point of fainting; or had taken a knock-out blow herself.

Bert Hopkins went up to her and smacked her gently on her cheek.

'I wish my corsets wasn't so tight,' she said vaguely. Then as she recovered herself, she folded her arms over his shoulders, and buried her head in his chest.

While he comforted her, the bird-catcher crawled on hands and knees towards the door. The docker, with a contemptuous glance, let him go.

'Come on, ole girl. Pull yerself together. We'll find the boy. He can't be far away.'

'Oh, Bert, I'm so ashamed.'

'You couldn't know.'

'But I turned him out. Christ, I turned him out.'

VI

THE NIGHT THE SWELLS
CAME TO GREENWICH

RUN away to sea, that's what he was going to do. Just as
Peg Weekes said. He'd show them. He would come back
an admiral, with a cocked hat and gold lace and a sword.
He wasn't afraid. Not Peter.

But he was. Plunging through the fog towards the riverbank, tortured by the injustice that had been done to him,
he needed somebody, anybody, to relieve the black hate
seething inside him. If people treated him that way, he could
hurt, too. He wished he had a cutlass, or that fishmonger's
knife, so that he could carve them into bloody bits like the
salmon. He thought that he would enjoy hurting people: it
would show them that he mattered, too.

In the murk he walked into a lamp-post and eased his
frustration by hitting back at it impotently with the back of
his hand. He picked up a stone and, when he couldn't spot
anything to break with it, stored it in his pocket; it instilled
in him a sense of bravado. Hugging the walls of the buildings, he made his way more by feel than by sight. Without
consciously considering where he was heading for, he
skirted a hostelry on the riverbank near the pier.

The taproom of the 'Ship' was one of the places
frequented by the Jack Collegemen; but, at that hour and

on that night, it was closed. Pretending that he didn't care, pretending that he didn't care about anything anymore, he walked on; coughing as the acrid air, billowing in a yellow cloud about him, stung his throat and brought water to his eyes. He went on to search out the inn called the 'Trafalgar' at the extremity of the riverside walk of the hospital. In the black mood he was in he wouldn't admit a reason; but it was another place where Peg Weekes, when he had any money, was a regular customer.

Surprisingly, the 'Trafalgar' was still awake. As he approached it, a glow of gaslight suffused the haze. He was drawn towards it like an insect: but he didn't venture too near. Gingerly circling the building he descended a flight of greasy steps to the water's edge. Even at that late hour the bow windows overlooking the Thames were filled with light, illuminating the name TRAFALGAR painted in bold black letters along the length of the river wall. The leaded panes offered an ideal target for his stone; but, as he toyed with the notion, curiosity got the better of him.

Something unexpected was going on. A barge, its hatch-ways carpeted with red cloth and with a gangplank leading up to one of the windows of the inn, was moored alongside. Using it as an improvised pier a steamer, decked out in flags and awnings, lay with her stem pointing upstream.

In the quiet he could hear the murmur of conversation in the rooms. Through the fog he could see the shadows of the assembly moving about behind the windows. Calf-deep in the mud, a shrimp pressed against the baulks of the river wall, he watched and listened intently. Not realising what it was all about, he knew enough to recognise that this was one of the occasions when the swells had come to Green-wich.

That night, such is the way of chance, Lord Palmerston had brought the members of his Government down the river from Westminster to enjoy the traditional supper of white-bait at the 'Trafalgar.' Delayed to some degree by the fog, and to an even greater measure by the excellence of the port, the party had lasted late into the night. That night Peg Weekes, as a veteran of Nelson's navy, was presented to the Prime Minister who gave him a sovereign to drink the Queen's health. As Peter sheltered under the wall, Peg himself reeled out of the 'Trafalgar' towards his berth in the hospital and, after a few yards, sat down with a satisfied bump on the road.

'Struck, b'God,' he bumbled bemusedly.

Then, raising his quavering voice as if he were calling over a high wind, he sang out: 'Boarding parties ready. Stand by to board.'

Foundering on his back, his sticks scattered as wildly as the spars of a craft in a storm, his wooden leg splayed like a useless mast, his tricorn hat tumbled over his nose, he swore in the nautical jargon of a generation before.

To Peter's sharp ears, Peg's voice sounded with the insistence of a distant siren. Eagerly, he swarmed up the river steps. Sensing direction, he put himself at the old boy's side.

'Peg.'

On his knees he endeavoured to push him into a sitting position.

'I've lost m'rudder, matey.'

'It's me, Peg. It's Peter.'

'Any port in a storm. I've dowsed m'glim and I'm all broached-to. Give me a quid, he did. Old Pam hisself. "Weekes," sez he, "the Royal Navy is proud of Hearts of

Oak like you"; and he sinks an oar into his breeches and, drawing out a long silk purse, drops me a sovereign. What are you doing, matey, pushing me about?'

'I'm trying to help you, Peg.'

'You're trying to turn me out of m'hammock, that's what you're doing.'

Testily, he thrust Peter aside.

'The other toffs shook hands with me as well. Never been such an object of attention since they seized me up on the gratings.'

He pulled Peter towards him again.

'Do you know summat?' he confided, with a knowing tap on the side of his nose. 'I ain't got the holler legs I used to have when I were a topman. I'm all broached-to.'

His words scrambled into a fuddled mutter. Peter could make no impression on him. It appeared that he was hard aground for the night.

On an impulse he snatched Peg's hat. He made for the river and, wading through the mud, filled it to the brim with water. Cupping the crown in both hands he succeeded in getting back without spilling more than half of it. The rest he emptied over Peg. As the cold douche sluiced on his head he stirred like a ship on a flooding tide. Floating back into consciousness he windmilled his arms as if he were engaging some imaginary adversary. Then, with a puzzled shake of his head, he succeeded in raising himself on his elbows.

'I will now sing a few staves,' he announced.

'You mustn't, Peg; they'll find us out.'

'Silence between decks.'

With a preposterous dignity, the old man filled his lungs and started to sing:

> *'There is a fountain filled with blood*
> *Drawn from Emmanuel's veins . . .'*

He got no further. Desperately, Peter smothered the noise by pressing his hand over his mouth.

'Wha's the matter?'

'Peelers, Peg!'

It was a false alarm; but it was a phrase that had usually worked with Pa. The intensity of his tone, the sobering effect of a word that could only mean trouble, roused Peg as well. He plunged about, fishing for his sticks, while Peter got behind him and heaved. Breathing heavily, Peg achieved a sitting position. He could do no more.

'Anchor's fouled, matey. You'll have to cast off without me. Where do you hail from?'

'I keep on telling you, Peg. Don't you know me? I'm Peter.'

'Then why didn't you say so? No you ain't. You ain't Peter. That's Pa Smelley's boy, the one the Peelers are arter . . . You ain't Peter, he's gone.'

'Can't you see it's me?'

Peg shook his head vaguely.

'So help me. I'm all broached-to. Gave me a jimmy o' goblin he did. "Splice the mainbrace," sez he. So I did.'

'You ain't listening, Peg. I ain't got nowhere to go to. Polly won't 'ave me neither.'

'You been to see Polly?'

'She won't 'ave me. I ain't got nowhere to go to. You got to listen to me.'

In his agitation he dragged on Peg's arm.

'Can't you find somewhere to hide me . . . afore the Peelers get me?'

'Can't even see you. Is it m'old eyes, or are we fog-bound?'

'It's a fog.'

'Then that's the time to stow away; when they can't see you creep aboard. That's what I said to Pa Smelley's boy. Fine upstanding lad he was. Stow away, I said.'

He sniffed sentimentally. His head lolled and, once again, he sank flat on his back on the cobbles. For a while, Peter crouched beside him in the bewilderment of a dog unrecognised even by its own familiars. He had hoped so much when he found Peg. Now, there was no one.

He might have remained with him until he came round; but his vigil was disturbed by approaching footsteps. Warily, he backed away. Pressing his hands into the brick-work of the street wall he again edged towards the river steps; and waited.

'Cwikey, a corpse.'

'I vow you're right, Bertie.'

Two young men, elegantly attired in evening-cloaks, with white gloves and silk hats tipped over their noses, bent down enquiringly. One of them employed his gold-mounted cane to give Peg an exploratory prod in the ribs. In answer he emitted a protesting grunt.

'He don't sound dead. Strike a lucifer, old horseman.'

'Sure he won't catch fire? He weeks like a wum puncheon.'

The two laughed. They had had a convivial evening themselves. Fumbling with the matches they made several boss-shots before succeeding in holding a flame fairly steadily over Peg's prostrate carcass. In the fashion of the times, they themselves were luxuriantly whiskered; gilded youths, they had been in attendance, in some junior capacity, on the Ministers of the Crown.

'Gad, Bertie, it's the old tar; don't you know, the one the First Lord presented to the P.M. What a lark. I say, what do you say to getting him under sail again?'

'Yes, let's twy and float him off.'

Exuberantly, they busied themselves getting Peg upright. Then each of them drew one of his arms across their shoulders and lifted him off the ground.

'I say, Bertie, this is rich. Now we've salvaged him what are we going to do with the body?'

'What shall we do with the dwunken sailor?'

They both took up the tune of the shanty.

> *'What shall we do with the drunken sailor,*
> *early in the morning?'*

Peg, stirred by the familiar chorus, began singing as well. From the steps, Peter saw them prop him against a wall while they recovered his hat and sticks. One of the revellers crowned Peg with his own topper and himself adopted the tricorn. Supporting him on both sides they guided him dizzily away.

'What you need, gran'papa, is some of the hair of the dog that bit you. Where shall we set course for, Bertie?'

'What about the jolly old "Fortune of War?"'

'Suppose the steamer goes without us?'

'Shouldn't think Pam will miss us, what?'

'Come on, Bertie, let's make a proper night of it.'

'Yes, let's have a pwoper night out.'

Defiantly, Peter hurled his stone as the voices of the two exquisites trailed away into the distance. It passed near enough to cause them to duck and, with a tinkle of glass, holed a ground floor window.

'Cwikey, where did that come from?'

'Was it one of your shipmates, gran'papa?'

Peg slowly turned his head, and stared behind him.

'Peter,' he called.

But the gleam of comprehension had come too late. His two companions bundled him away from the scene of the mischief as Peter himself bolted, unhearingly, instinctively, for the river. The aggressiveness that had possessed him, the determination to show them, had been his undoing. In panic, his legs ruled his mind.

Scrambling on to the bank, he searched out one of the cables mooring the barge. Hand over hand, with the ease of a monkey, he shinned up it and heaved himself on to the deck. No one noticed him wriggling across the hatchways or saw him drop over the rails of the steamer. During that miserable night the crew, waiting for the bigwigs to finish their party, had gone below to the warmth of the forward cabin. The gaily decorated vessel, its open-work bell-mouthed funnel steaming sleepily, its paddle-boxes ornamented with the arms of the City of London, was temporarily unguarded.

There was nowhere to hide on the open deck. Stealing aft he peered hopefully down a companionway into a pool of soft reflected light. He cocked an ear, but there wasn't a whisper of anyone moving. Resting both hands on the brass rail he tiptoed below.

He found himself in a lobby adjoining a saloon. The door was ajar. Inside, a liveried footman was stretched in a doze along one of two banquettes which extended the length of the cabin. Peter hardly noticed him. As he peered round the door he was dazzled by a vision of silver and white napery, of crystal and ruby glasses, bowls of flowers, baskets of fruit, pyramids of cold collations; all glittering in the illumination of pink-shaded candelabra, set in the airless luxury of red velvet upholstery and polished woodwork. For the reception of its distinguished passengers, the saloon of the penny steamer—normally as unwelcoming as the inside of a third-class railway compartment—had been transformed.

To Peter, it was as mysterious and unreal as a peep-show. He shrank back, overwhelmed by the wonder of it; so much to eat, so many lights, so much that was clean and white.

It was his first glimpse of the world that Disraeli had said was 'for the few and the very few.' Peter, like a sinner at the gates of heaven, realised that he had transgressed. He drew into the shadows behind the door.

He sank back into heavy curtains which covered a rack of shelves used for hats and coats and baggage; and, at the same moment, his heart sank with him. As the curtains parted under his weight, he heard the beginnings of a hubbub of activity on the deck above. With a squeeze he cramped himself into the lower shelf and listened, with a pounding heart, as the oscillating engine raised the head of steam.

He had watched it all happen so often that he recognised every sound and footstep on the iron deck; the call-boy shouting the skipper's hand-signalled orders to the engine-room; the thump of the mooring-ropes and the fenders as they were stowed aboard; the tread of the passengers towards the awning abaft the paddle-boxes; the tremble that ran through the vessel as the great wheels that drove her started to life. But, although he had heard the names of the places that the steamers plied between—London Bridge, the Tower, the Pool, Westminster—he had never seen them, not even in books.

That night the swells didn't loiter on deck. As the steamer got under way, they trooped below in little groups, conversing with the studied ease of men who made an art of talk; whose tongues were lubricated with vintage wine and old brandy, and who had the deep-set shoulders built for punishment which distinguishes statesmen, like professional pugilists, from others with qualities more easily vulnerable than their own.

As they arrived in the lobby the footman, stirred from his slumbers, received their hats and overcoats and, breaking the curtains over Peter's hiding-place, decorously ordered the apparel on the shelves. Starting at the top, there was no cause for him to look down at the bundle of rags on the level of his white stockings and buckled shoes.

Peter watched the tightly trousered legs in an unhurried procession into the saloon while the footman kept his eye on the companionway to assess the precise degree of obsequiousness to be accorded to each of the new arrivals. The Duke of Newcastle and Lord John Russell, the Foreign Secretary; Lord Herbert and Mr Milner Gibson, who had been persuaded to accept the Board of Trade; Sir George Cornwall Lewis and Mr William Cowper—members of a Cabinet that contained 'at least a couple of men who had been Prime Ministers, and as many more who thought they ought to be'—filed through, each adding his own quota, as the shelves filled, to the discovery of a frightened boy.

Gladstone was there; but, with sleek black hair and an ascetic face still relatively unlined, the Chancellor of the Exchequer appeared no more formidable than any other of his colleagues. The footman seemed to find him rather less so. Mr Gladstone had to affect to clear the fog out of his throat in order to emphasise his presence.

'An inclement night,' he remarked austerely.

'Like the Budget proposals, Chancellor,' said a genial voice behind him. 'Lacking in vision.'

'My portfolio, as you well know, Prime Minister, is at your disposal.'

'Ah . . . ah . . . ah . . . Not again!'

Characteristically, the Prime Minister was the last to leave the open deck. In his middle seventies, Lord Palmerston was still a demon for fresh air and exercise, and time hadn't withered a boyish delight in poking fun. He loved teasing Gladstone, who bore himself like a misunderstood prelate and who, indeed, was suspected by Disraeli of being one in disguise. On this occasion, the Chancellor didn't deign to reply. Stalking into the saloon, as if he were dividing the House of Commons, he made way—not for the first time and for much longer than he cared to remember—for a Prime Minister who wore high office with the jaunty ease that he wore his clothes.

The footman, who was Lord Palmerston's personal servant, bowed low—partly to hide a smile of approbation—as his master handed over his white gloves and his celebrated white top hat. Helped out of his overcoat he revealed a trim figure, tightly buttoned in square-cut green cloth with a high collar bound with a black silk cravat. He had a big head with heavy white side-whiskers and a deep voice.

As he shot his cuffs, and arranged his cravat, the footman bent down to find a fitting place for his hat and coat. With an astounded stare he spotted Peter. The Prime Minister, resting his hands on his knees, got down to look, too.

'Upon my soul, Evans, what's that?'

'I dunno, my lord,' replied Evans grimly. 'But we'll soon find out.'

He ran his hand over the trembling frame as if he were tickling a trout. Then, with thumb and forefinger, he gripped firmly on an ear. Squirming with terror, Peter was pulled out of his hole. Evans, holding him at arm's length, endeavoured to resume his posture of unruffled dignity.

'Would you care to leave this little matter to me, m'lord?' he enquired hopefully.

'Ah . . . ah . . . ah . . . no, I'm interested.'

'One of the lower orders, I fear, m'lord.'

'That's self-evident.'

'Must 'ave crept aboard somehow.'

'When you were sleeping, eh, Evans?'

'No, m'lord.'

'You always do.'

'It got very late, m'lord.'

Evans' face reddened to the colour of his own satin breeches. Palmerston's eyes were twinkling. Peering through the saloon door at the gathering of his ministers he interrupted the conversation.

'We have an unexpected guest, gentlemen.'

Meanwhile, Peter was trying to escape. Evans launched a kick at him which he hoped wouldn't be noticed, and missed. The ministers closed towards the door to find out what was going on. With a smile, Palmerston indicated the catch.

'Looks like one of Disraeli's discarded waistcoats, Sir George. But inside it, unbelievable as it may appear, beats the heart of a human being. Pray let him go, Evans.'

'He's a little devil, m'lord. He'll 'ave at you.'

'Let him go.'

Peter backed into a corner.

'Why did you come aboard this boat?' Palmerston enquired gently. 'Was it because you have nowhere of your own to go to?'

Peter could only gulp. A carefully modulated voice, coldly accusing, intervened:

'Has he stolen anything?'

'It could be, Gladstone, that he has stolen the Channel Forts. Personally, I prefer to give him the benefit of the doubt. Kindly leave me alone with him awhile, gentlemen . . .'

A little crestfallen, the others retreated behind the closed door of the saloon to remark, not for the first time, on the quixotic behaviour of their chief. Peter clung to the shadows.

'Do you know who I am?' Palmerston said.

He looked up at the face, delineated by history, in its silver frame of flowing hair. He peered into the deep-set eyes in which the crows' feet were angled in the line of laughter. He felt a little less afraid. He almost found his voice again.

'No, guv,' he whispered.

'There's every reason why you shouldn't know my name. What's yours, boy?'

'Peter.'

'What's your other name, Peter?'

'Ain't got one.'

'You mean you haven't got a father or a mother. Who have you got?'

'There was Pa, but he's drownded. There's Pol, but she's chucked me out. I ain't got nobody now.'

'No home to go to?'

'I asked Peg, but he was drunk.'

Under the kindly eye, the hypnotic voice, he was gaining confidence.

'Who's Peg?'

'He fought with Nelson at Trafalgar.'

'He was drunk, was he?'

'Course 'e was. A swell called Pam gave him a sovereign.'

Palmerston's face wrinkled in laughter.

'I'm Pam,' he said. 'So I'm the one who's responsible for getting you into trouble. How old are you?'

'Dunno.'

'Come nearer, and tell me what the trouble is.'

'I caught a salmon with Pa: but nobody wouldn't believe me.'

'Where did you catch him?'

'Off Dead Man's Island.'

'In the Thames?'

'Yes, guv.'

'Must have been another sort of fish. Never mind. Why, you're trembling. You're cold, too. Are you hungry?'

'Yes, guv.'

The quiet exchange between the greatest man in England and one of the most insignificant of Her Majesty's subjects was interrupted by the precipitate entrance of the skipper of the steamboat.

'M'lord!'

'Yes, skipper.'

'They say there's a stowaway aboard.'

'If you're referring to this child, he's my guest. You'll be serving us better, skipper, by resuming your duties.'

In the saloon, Lord John Russell was enquiring of the

Commissioner of Works and Buildings what was the matter with his damn clock last night; commenting that, as Big Ben seemed to be striking all hours at all hours, it was fortunate that it had been christened after a Commissioner of Works and not, as originally proposed, Royal Victoria after the Queen. Otherwise, the Government's relations with Osborne might be even more unpredictable, if that were possible, than they were. In a very brief interval they had all conveniently forgotten the P.M.'s eccentric concern over a foundling.

When Palmerston ushered him into the saloon, sheltering him under his arm as if he were his guest at a soirée, it wasn't only Gladstone who muttered that the old man was at last showing signs of senile decay. When he settled Peter on a seat in the corner, the company winced perceptibly.

'Bring the boy some cold mutton and apple pie, Evans. Some negus, too, he needs it. And . . . ah, ah, ah . . . give him a good helping.'

The old man's interest in the welfare of the working classes, and especially of children, had been notorious ever since he had been Home Secretary in Lord Shaftesbury's administration. But this was carrying charity a little too far; exposing ministers of the Crown to the risk of cholera and contact with who could tell what other pestilence beside. The boy wasn't merely filthy; he was stinking.

If he overheard the whispers, Palmerston's poise was impenetrable. He serenely poured himself a glass of port.

Peter twisted and lowered his head uncomprehendingly, hardly daring to look at the delicacies that were spread in front of him. He rubbed his hands on his closed knees as suspiciously as if he were faced with the baited plate of a jawed trap. He drew in his shoulders to make himself as small as possible. Outside, in the benevolent half-darkness, he was frightened enough. Now, he was caught in the grip of a bad dream, encircled by questing hostile faces, trapped in a blinding light from which he couldn't escape.

'Aren't you going to eat it now you've got it?'

Evans, glaring down at him, assumed the shape of a red devil. With an involuntary cry, he threw himself on the door and ran out, up the companionway, into the blessed oblivion of the night. He would have jumped overboard; but one of the hands grabbed him as he threw his legs over the rail. Too tired to struggle he collapsed on to the iron deck.

'Bring him some brandy.'

Palmerston himself was beside him with other ministers who had run ahead of their chief to avert a tragedy; and, more important perhaps, a possible scandal and unfavourable comment by Delane in *The Times*.

'What went wrong?'

'You would have thought that the urchin would have been flattered.'

'He was hungry, wasn't he?'

'Perhaps the negus went to his head.'

'No, I was watching him; he didn't drink it.'

'Well, it only proves what I've always insisted. If you cosset the poor they'll kick you in the teeth.'

'Ah . . . ah . . . ah . . . I must remind you, gentlemen, that he's a very small boy.'

The Prime Minister paused solicitously as Peter was lifted into one of the slatted seats which furnished the deck. Then, with another grunt, almost as if he was talking to himself, he went on.

'Illiterate, starving, homeless, deprived of the affections

of a father or a mother; a dependant of a country which aspires to the conduct of the affairs of an Empire. Before God, he and his like are the charge of Her Majesty's Government and Her Majesty's ministers.'

'I must remind you, Prime Minister, that there are prior claims on the Treasury's resources.'

'Prior claims?'

'The Channel Forts, for example.'

'We found three million to build Mr Bazelgette's sewers.'

'Five million,' corrected the Chancellor.

'Then, if we can spend five million on the Thames, we should be able to vote the revenue to care for starvelings like this on the banks.'

'But the State already provides plenty of admirable institutions to which paupers can go. Charity schools, casual wards, workhouses . . .'

'I recollect that, when I was Home Secretary, a national fast was recommended as an expedient to deal with the scourge of cholera. An outlook as bleak as yours, my friend; as bleak as the prospects of this child.'

'While I sympathise with the sentiment, I must emphasise, with the greatest respect, Prime Minister, that we cannot afford to give these important social problems the consideration they deserve while you yourself insist on the expenditure of vast sums on purely military projects.'

'Try as you will, Gladstone, I am not prepared to expose this country unarmed to her enemies.'

'In that event, you have done yourself, and this child, a disservice by introducing him to a manner of life for which he is unfitted and to which he can never attain. What's going to happen to him now?'

'So far, Gladstone, you have never given me cause to

doubt your integrity or . . . ah . . . ah . . . your selfless disinterest in other people. What's going to happen to the boy
now? Dammit, I'll keep the Channel Forts and I'll keep him,
too. I'll take him back to Cambridge House with me.'

'You won't do that?'

'I can, sir, and, by God, I will.'

The fog was lifting as the steamer bumped gently into
the landing-stage at the southern end of Westminster Bridge.
A line of broughams, their lamps gleaming along the road,
waited to take the various ministers to their houses. To his
disgust, and to the waiting constables' surprise, Evans was
deputed to escort Peter.

'Not such a bad night, after all. You take the boy to
Cambridge House in my brougham, Evans. I'll ride, and
get some exercise.'

'What am I to tell her ladyship, m'lord?'

'Tell her I'm on my way and send the boy below stairs
for a good wash and some clean clothes. Then put him to
bed.'

With an elegant lift of his white hat to his colleagues, the
Prime Minister mounted the grey horse which was always
in readiness for him. As he trotted off, alone, his Cabinet
looked after him; some wondering how long he could last,
some hoping that the old veteran couldn't carry on much
longer. But, tonight, his back was straight and his seat as
firm as a young man's.

With a fatalistic shrug of his shoulders to the coachman,
Evans pushed Peter into the brougham as the ministers
started to call their own. In the box of buttoned leather-
work, dark and stuffy, they travelled over Westminster
Bridge into Whitehall. Within a few minutes, lulled by the

sway of the carriage and the rhythmic clatter of the horse's hooves, Peter nodded. Utterly exhausted, physically and emotionally, he fell into a troubled half-sleep.

In Piccadilly, the coachman passed the pairs of wrought-iron gates linking the circular drive to the main entrance of the mansion. Instead, he took the turning down the side of Cambridge House to the stables and kitchens in Whitehorse Street, pulling up outside the back entrance.

As Evans got out, giving Peter a shake to wake him, he looked down in his cockaded hat from the eminence of his box.

'My compliments to 'is little lordship,' he grinned. 'We're 'ere.'

Evans had to lift him on to the pavement. He stood there, bleary-eyed, only half-awake to the clang of the bell sounding in the servants' hall. There was a noisy unloosing of bolts and chains behind the iron-barred doors. With a guffaw, the coachman drew off as Evans pushed him into a subterranean passage.

An elderly servant, with a shawl over her shoulders, a mob-cap over her hair and a bunch of keys at her waist, stood on the threshold. She took one startled look at the scarecrow who had invaded her domain.

'Lawks!' she exclaimed.

VII

POOR POL

DULLY, like a reflection in a pewter pot, daylight came to end the leaden hours in which she had tried to sleep. Face down on her mattress, Polly was stirring uncomfortably in a sweat which stickied her nightdress and straggled her fair hair in dank tails. There had been no rest for her; only half-conscious intervals in a vigil of staring wakefulness and remorse.

Time after time, she had tossed the bedclothes on to the floor and then, trembling, drawn them back. In her fever, her mind was crowded with images; the faces, monstrous and distorted, of Pa Smelley, the bird-catcher, Peg Weekes, the two toffs and the constables, surging mockingly towards her, grimacing horribly and exchanging identity until she swam with nausea. When she cried out she could hear the disembodied voice of Bert Hopkins answering; but he seemed very far away. Worst of all, she had been haunted by a vision of Peter—dead mostly—floating just out of reach of her questing arms.

But that night that had seemed to last for ever she hadn't been in bed long. The arrival of Peg Weekes, after he had been walked sober enough by the toffs to have a recollection of his encounter with Peter outside the 'Trafalgar,' had sent her hurrying to the riverside. Bert Hopkins went with her; and, when Peg went to sleep on a bed of sacks, the toffs, for a bit of a lark, came too. But it was a wild goose chase. The toffs wandered off in search of other game. She had returned, distrait and hysterical, with Bert trying, clumsily and uncomprehendingly, to comfort her. He couldn't understand that she just wanted him to go away.

She didn't recognise herself what had happened to her; but the sudden yearning for Peter, the explosion of emotion precipitated by the events of the night, the odd sense of physical aversion she had felt for Bert Hopkins, all stemmed from the same cause. When she dragged her legs out of bed, mussing her tousled hair and drawing down her crumpled nightdress, she knew that she was going to be sick.

Every morning, it was Polly's first duty to carry the takings of the previous day to the landlord of the 'Fortune of War.' He was seldom on the premises. To the customers, he was a fleeting figure, only appearing occasionally to hang about, spider-like, behind the bar. It was said that he had other, more disreputable, interests to engage his attention.

For her board and keep, and fifteen pounds a year, with the assistance of a cellarman who was usually drunk, Polly slaved on her own. It was a small pub and, over the years, the money she took, and handed over, had shown that she was an honest servant. That day, she locked away the cash carefully in a place where the landlord could find it for himself.

She collected her own small savings from underneath her mattress. She packed her clothes, with such possessions as she had, in a carpet bag. Then, wrapping a shawl purposefully about her shoulders, she went to find Peg Weekes. He was snoring noisily.

'Wake up, Peg.'

'Where am I? I've lost m'compass.'

'You've got to go back to the Hospital.'

Complaining testily he reluctantly accepted his sticks and dragged himself to his feet. Polly clapped on his hat for him. With a last pale-faced glance at the little bar-parlour, she propped him on his way through a stone-floored passage to a back door. She locked it as they left, returning the key by pushing it through a crack over the doorstep. Then, with Peg at her side, she fled the 'Fortune of War.'

The fog had lifted. It was late enough in the morning for the streets to be filling. The traffic was again crowding the river. Pressing on Peg's arm, she tried to hustle him.

'Can't make sail any faster, Pol. M'old stump's aching fit to burst.'

She stopped.

'I got to find Peter.'

Her voice was as expressionless as a sleepwalker's.

'Peter? You won't find him. Stowed away to sea, that's what he's done, same as I said. Peter, sez I . . .'

'You saw him last night when you was broached. He can't have run away to sea, not yet. Where did he go to?'

'Where the Peelers can't find him, o'course. Peter, sez I . . .'

'Come on.'

She guided him to Greenwich Pier where the up-river steamers were taking on passengers. She watched eagerly while baggage was stowed, families shepherded aboard, and middle-class papas, on their way to city counting-houses, settled down with ivory knives to cut the pages of the

morning's newspapers. It had seemed the first obvious place
to look for him. But, as her eyes travelled restlessly over the
activity on the wharf and the craft bustling up and down
the tideway, she was reminded how very small Peter was;
and London, how big. Not that she was deterred. However
far she had to search, however long, she had to find him.
She had arrived at a state of emotional instability in which
he was necessary to her own female completeness.

'I'm going now, Peg.'

'Where?'

'On the steamer.'

'What for?'

'How do I know what for?' she said wildly. 'I'm going,
that's what.'

Clutching her carpet bag, floridly patterned with cabbage
roses, she left him. Propped on his sticks, Peg just stood;
too old, too lost in the past, too bewildered to understand.
She found a seat in the bow where she could keep a watch
on both banks. She sat there, still and remote, without so
much as a glance over her shoulder, as the penny steamer
pulled away.

She felt sure that he wouldn't stray from the river. The
river had spawned him, its mud had been his playground,
and its waters had lapped him every day of his life since he
could walk. As the paddle-boat plied upstream she looked
for him on the trains of barges, among the mudlarks like
himself on the tideline of every reach, on the crowded
wharves and piers, anywhere where the gulls squawked and
quarrelled and where a boy might be competing with them
for the loot. On any other occasion, her eyes would have
been dancing at the unfolding panorama of London; but
her attention never wandered. Hugging the carpet-bag over

the billowing balloon of her crinoline, she looked carefully at any urchin who showed.

At the Tower, she even thought she saw him, playing with other boys in the water. Excitedly, she left the steamer at the pier and went to the river's edge. When she discovered that it wasn't Peter, she got on a boat sailing the other way. She could so easily have missed him among all the craft and people. She travelled up-river and down-river, always sitting well in the prow, where she could see better, until the clerks in the pier ticket offices and the crews on the decks began to recognise her. She was too pretty a baggage to pass unnoticed for long. At first, they whistled after her appreciatively. Later, a kindly waterman came to her and asked if anything was wrong. She shook her head non-committally and, at the next stop, changed steamers to get away from him.

She lost all sense of time. She had no appetite and no thirst. She just had a sensation, as the hours dragged on, of dull emptiness. She travelled backwards and forwards until it was almost too dark to see the banks. And, at last, she stumbled ashore at a stop on the Surrey side of which she didn't even know the name.

She went to the 'ladies only' bar of a pub, ignoring at first the friendly overtures of a group of crones seated in the mahogany-lined compartment. She drank gin-and-water until she was tipsy. She started giggling to herself. She giggled and hiccuped until she was near to tears. Then she lurched on her feet to go. One of the old women intervened.

'A nice girl like you, ducks, oughtn't to be out on the streets alone. Why don't you sit down and rest your plates for a bit? You look tired, dearie.'

She sat down out of necessity rather than choice.

'That's the way. Now tell us what went wrong. 'As the old man been bashin' you about?'

'Ain't married.'

'You ain't in the family way, are you?' With sure instinct, a toothless old hag looked at her conspiratorially. 'Because if you was, I might know someone what could 'elp a nice girl like you.'

'Don't want any help . . . wanna go to bed.'

She shook her head wearily.

'Where do you live?'

'Ain't living nowhere, not just now.'

With coos of interest, the women closed about her in a tighter ring. This was even better than they had hoped.

'You're not in trouble with the police, are you, ducks? Doesn't matter if you are. Not among us. We're friends.'

'Mrs 'Iggins 'ere has got a nice place which she lets to lodgers sometimes.'

'If they're select, that is. Wouldn't mind, understand, if you had a gentleman friend up sometimes, specially if he had a collar and tie. Is that your bag, dearie? My, it's a pretty one.'

'Mrs 'Iggins' place is only just round the corner. Eightpence a night, with breakfast. You've got some money, ain't you? But of course you 'ave. What about another little drink afore you go?'

Step by step, she yielded to the blandishments of the old women. But she locked the door of the tawdry bedroom, with its torn lace curtains, its tarnished mirrors, and stale human smells. Mrs Higgins, with visitors to recommend, knocked in vain. Early the following morning, she went back to the river. All that day and for days after, increasingly haggard and unkempt, she sailed up and down;

eating, when she had to, at whelk and coffee stalls, searching the dark corners of wharves and river steps, peering inside boats which were aground on the tide and, as time went on, desperately questioning bargees and dockers, men in the ship-breaking and shipbuilding yards, mudlarks and shoremen and even the crews on the steamers where she was now a familiar figure. Most of them laughed. A few tried to discourage her. But she was relentless.

At night, she drifted into doss-houses where, in unspeakable filth, practising every vice, boasting every crime, people slept, ten or twenty to a room, for a few pennies a night. Her own money was almost gone. As the days went by, her self-respect slipped too. Coarsened by the company she was keeping, increasingly reckless of her own appearance, she was changed into a ruthless, even dangerous, virago. In her more violent moments she was lucky to escape arrest. In her quieter ones, she was cowed and infinitely suspicious. At first, when she travelled up and down the river, the young men had manœuvred to sit beside her. Now, she infested the steamers; respectable passengers drawing away from her for more distant seats.

She struck up an acquaintance with the gangs who made their living making forays into the sewers. The toshers crawled at low tide into the sewer entrances, working for miles through the pestilential passages, searching the sludge for nails, old rope and bones; and sometimes chancing on richer booty like coins, bits of plate and silver spoons. Polly, in her degradation, helped them to divide and parcel the loot. But she never stopped looking for Peter.

It was because she was now notorious on the waterfront that Peg Weekes was able to find her so easily. On the day that he was seated importantly on one of the penny steamers himself and received a greeting of welcome, as befitted an old sailor, from the skipper, there was no need for special enquiry. Everyone on the quayside at Greenwich, and many more, knew of the goings-on of the barmaid of the 'Fortune of War'; although she had never journeyed so far down-stream again.

The hands on the steamers saw her regularly. But she had done no wrong—the landlord of the 'Fortune of War' admitted that she hadn't stolen anything—it was a free country and it was rumoured that, when one of her old customers had gone after her to try and woo her back, she had seen him off with a flea in his ear and a black eye.

But this time it was different. Peg Weekes had been entrusted with a mission by none other than the Prime Minister himself. A gentleman with lavender gloves and a gold watch-chain, who was introduced as a member of Lord Palmerston's household, had arrived, with other officials, to summon him to the Governor's room at the Hospital.

They had asked him questions about old Pa Smelley and his fishing. Over a decanter of madeira, they had invited his personal opinion as to whether he thought it possible that, with the improved condition of the river as a consequence of the construction of the new sewers, salmon were running again. They had enquired about Peter. Oiled with the wine, combined with a rusty memory, he had talked like a Dutch uncle; protesting that he had always said that the river was alive with fish, same as it had been in Admiral Nelson's time; insisting that he had seen the actual salmon which Peter had netted; and adding how much the boy, fine upstanding lad that he was, had benefited from his own instruction.

None of the smiling officials believed a word of it. But they were satisfied that Peter had caught a salmon. All the evidence collected by the police, they said, confirmed it. Further, they confidently anticipated that, when the intercepting sewers were completed, there would be many more fish in the future. They were all very pleased with themselves.

That was not all. Peter's story, he was told, had reached the ears of the Prime Minister and it was his personal wish that Peg Weekes, and a lady named Polly, should be informed that the boy was well cared for. Peter was now a member of the household staff at Cambridge House.

The officials had gone on to suggest that, since any intervention by the police might be misconstrued, Peg Weekes himself, as a pensioner of Her Majesty's navy, should undertake the delicate mission of reassuring the lady in question. Peg Weekes touched his forelock, and came away richer by another sovereign.

As the steamer stopped at the various landing-stages, sometimes as she passed others sailing in the opposite direction, the crew helped by hollering for news of the old hag—they used other epithets as well—on Peg's behalf. At last, one of the boats answered that they'd turned her off at the Tower. Peg's search ended soon after he began to make enquiries on the pier.

An individual, clad in a greasy velveteen coat and canvas trousers, with slops for shoes, edged towards him and, without saying anything, gave a significant toss of his head. He moved off, with a hint of a signal to Peg to follow him, into the narrow streets adjoining the river-front. It was in the district between the Docks and Rosemary Lane where, in a mess of slums, the most wretched had their dwellings.

At last, leaning against a wall, picking his teeth with a copper nail, the guide waited for Peg to join him.

'What do you want 'er for?'

'Private and personal,' said Peg importantly.

'Yer won't find much of neither here, sailor.'

The man spat. Not to be outdone, Peg expectorated neatly on the same spot.

'Not bad for an old 'un,' admitted the other grudgingly. 'What's her game ganging up with us toshers here? Sez she was a barmaid down in Greenwich, she sez. Talks about a boy she's looking for. If it's hers, you'd think she'd be glad to be rid of the brat. Another chap came after her, and he was lucky to get away without being black-jacked. Know 'im?'

The tosher seemed more eager to extract information than to give it. A group of scarecrows gathered to stare at Peg's uniform. After a lifetime in the hell of the lower deck of a wooden ship of the line, he was undismayed.

'What you want, cap'n?'

'He's lookin' for the woman what's working with Nasty-face's lot.'

The tosher gave the information without moving and without withdrawing the point of the copper nail from the gaps in his teeth. The others crowded in the more.

'I wonder what'll 'appen if we take the ole beggar's sticks away from 'im?'

'Garn, leave 'im alone. He can't do any harm.'

The street was seething now with people, popping to the surface from every hole and cranny, like denizens of a nest of insects. A mob of youths, in tight trousers and long coats, with shaggy mops of hair, began to finger the wide lapels of Peg's coat. Standing his ground, he swept one of his sticks

over their grinning faces. At once, they toppled him off
his remaining leg.

In the uproar that followed, such a mass of humanity
was packed about him that he was out of sight. It could
only have been a matter of time before he was trampled
to death. They had already started fighting among themselves.

It may have been that somebody, overhearing what was
said by Peg and the tosher, had sloped off to drop Polly the
wink. It may have been that she herself, like the others, had
been drawn from her rat-hole simply to investigate the
cause of the commotion. But she appeared. Flailing a way
through the swaying rabble, using her fingernails like meat
hooks whenever she found bare flesh, she fought her way to
Peg's side.

She was quickly joined by a man whose face had been
horribly mutilated by some accident. Wielding a short stout
stick he cleared a circle. Polly helped Peg to his feet. He
was shaken but, astonishingly, self-possessed.

'Scum! Landlubberly scum!'

Fortunately, in the free-for-all, nobody was listening.

'You shouldn't 'ave come here,' Polly said breathlessly.
'Why can't you leave me be?'

'I got news for you.'

'About Peter?'

'He's found.'

'Is he dead?'

'No, Pol.'

'Then where is he? Go on, don't stand there staring at me.
I know what you're thinking. Tell me where he is.'

Peg pressed his fingers knowingly to his nose and plainly
looked about for somewhere more peaceful to converse.

Polly dragged him into another alley which was relatively tranquil.

'We can talk here.'

'I've got a message for you, Pol, a message with the compliments of the Prime Minister. Just think o' that.'

'What's he got to do with the likes of us? Where's Peter?'

'He's in the Prime Minister's mansion. That's where he is. Ole Pam told me so his very self. So there.'

'You're up to your story-telling again.'

'I ain't, Pol; not this time. Peg, sez Pam . . .'

'What's Peter doing in a swank place like that? How did he get in there?'

'He must have stowed away aboard the steamer at the 'Trafalgar,' same as I 'structed him. Peter, sez I . . .'

'Someone told you to come here and tell me the tale.'

'The swells come to Greenwich, Pol, special to tell me.'

'Bah!'

She tossed her head disbelievingly.

'What do swells want with a mudlark like him? If he's in this swell's mansion, where is it? Ho, ho, you tell me that. Where is it?'

'I ain't been in that part of London, not lately, I ain't. But 'most anybody knows where the Prime Minister lives.'

Through the clouded pupils of his old eyes Peg stared into hers unhappily.

'Ain't you coming back to Greenwich, Pol? The ole 'Fortune o' War' doesn't seem the same without you.'

'So that's it. Getting me back to Greenwich with a cock-and-bull story about Peter. Well, I ain't wearing it, see. You can tell 'em I ain't wearing it. You can tell Bert Hopkins, too, that he's well rid of me. He'll know what I mean.'

'What's going to happen to you, Pol?'

'How do I know.'

'Got any money?'

She shrugged.

'Maybe I can find summat you can have.'

She watched dully as Peg fumbled under his shirt and extracted a purse hanging on a leather thong about his neck. Unlacing it, he clumsily picked out a sovereign.

' 'Ere, take that.'

Turning his back to hide his embarrassment, he shoved the coin at her and, when at first she failed to take it, prodded her impatiently in the ribs.

'Go on, 'ave it.'

Not looking herself, Polly closed her hand over his big fist. When the sovereign, from such an unexpected source, dropped into her palm, it wasn't ingratitude but a gesture of long habit that she took the precaution of biting it to make sure that it was a good one. It wasn't often that the likes of Peg Weekes could produce a quid.

'Where did you get it?'

'Same as I said, Pol. The swells gave it to me when they told me about Peter.'

The explanation, so simply given, so plainly true, swayed Polly like a blow. She only kept her balance by taking hold of Peg's arm. He himself, still unaware of the implications for her of what he had said, shuffled uncomfortably. He was afraid that she was going to be soppy about the sovereign.

'You can give it back to me later,' he mumbled.

She was still finding her tongue. All the emotion that she had bottled inside herself—the gnawing reproaches, the self-pity, the shrill disbelief—had been emptied out of her by one chance remark. Peg Weekes couldn't invent sovereigns.

'So it's right,' she whispered.

‘ 'Course it's right,' Peg grumbled. 'You got it in you hand.'

'I mean about Peter.'

'Oh, him!'

'Why didn't you tell me?'

'But I did, didn't I?'

'And I didn't believe you.'

Increasingly worried by the catch in her voice, antic pating a squall, Peg looked about in the vague hope of find ing quieter waters.

'So he's really in the Prime Minister's mansion. And thought he was dead. And that I'd killed him. Let me kee the sovereign, Peg. I'll pay you back, honest I will. But I' be needing some new clothes, and a new hat, won't I?'

'Maybe.'

'I can't go to a mansion looking like this.'

Peg didn't conceal his amazement at the proposal.

'You ain't thinking o' that?'

'Why not?' she bridled.

'It's no place for our sort, Pol.'

'Then it's no place for Peter neither. I got to see him. Yo know that. He needs me . . . and I need him.'

The emphasis in her voice left no margin for argumen Anyhow, Peg was only too anxious to disengage. Peop were again collecting in the alley of the slum to stare them. Fearful of another scene, wagging his head ar murmuring something about the consequences of sailir in deep waters, he made off. With a sudden sense of isol tion, Polly took a step or two after him. But, on secor thoughts, she stopped, turning the sovereign in her hot har and starting to smooth her crumpled clothes.

When he got to the end of the alley, Peg looked back

search of her; but she was already gone. She had left him, as she had before, to take her own fateful course. But, this time, Peg himself was left not without purpose. He made back to Greenwich determined to see Bert Hopkins and to tell him all about it.

Finding Cambridge House was easy. Getting into it was more difficult than she had anticipated. At any time, a knot of people stood outside to watch the comings and goings of the great men and beautiful women of the realm; and to give Pam himself a cheer as he trotted his horse through the crush of Piccadilly towards the House of Commons and back again. But the constables were continuously on guard. Although they took no exception to the demurely dressed woman, in a new pork-pie hat with a neat little feather, who stared through the railings into the circular courtyard beyond the iron gates, it was plain that the way inside was closely guarded. Peter was as far out of Polly's reach as ever.

But, as she watched the broughams and the saddle-horses passing between the courtyard and the stables, the pattern of the establishment revealed itself. Outside the stables in Glasshouse Street, she surreptitiously watched the wasp-waistcoated grooms and cockaded coachmen. It wasn't long before she discovered the pub they frequented in Shepherd's Market.

The landlord's complexion was the bright red of a lobster, and he had eyes like a cooked lobster which stared out over a grog-blossom nose and a large drooping moustache. Seated with his stomach creased into a small table in the saloon bar, chewing a cigar and sipping a large brandy-and-soda, he looked her over with professional appreciation. Good bar-maids were difficult to come by, pretty barmaids brought in business. She submitted without protest to an amorous pinch and a leer of approval at her well-filled blouse. It was worth it. She was offered a trial, on a day's notice, if she didn't mind sharing a bedroom with another girl. She said she didn't mind.

Anyhow it wasn't long before the other girl stormed off in a tantrum. The new one, she said, was queering her pitch. After that, Polly ruled the 'Coach and Horses' as she had the 'Fortune of War.' Even the landlord was reluctant to venture liberties.

She made no direct enquiries about Peter. She knew that he was still in Cambridge House because, occasionally, she overheard talk about him. There was the time when, with burning ears, she learnt that he had tried to run away. A constable had brought him back ignominiously for a beating on the kitchen table. Not that he wasn't free to do as he liked; but in the aura of the world 'for the few and the very few,' it never occurred to the Peters, or the Pollys, that they had the right to exercise the choice.

Indirectly, she let it drop that she had known Peter when she was a barmaid in Greenwich. She passed the information as off-handedly as she could. But, as her reputation in the neighbourhood grew, she reckoned that somebody would talk about it in the servants' hall at Cambridge House. Her estimate was right.

Yet it was Bert Hopkins who first came back into her life. Primed by Peg Weekes, he searched her out; filling the bar with his broad shoulders, his deep gurgling voice and the belt hung loosely round his loins. Unperturbed by the strange company he was in, physically sure of himself, completely at ease, he chucked her gently under the chin.

'Hello, ducks. So I've found you at last. What made you run away from me?'

She returned his welcome with troubled eyes.

'You ought to ask me what I'll have, Pol. 'Ow about a nice bitter?'

As she pulled the pump, she watched him distractedly.

'Careful, or you'll empty the barrel,' he laughed.

'You shouldn't 'ave come here.'

'Why not?'

'Because.'

'Because you want Peter rather than me?'

'No, Bert.'

'Then what is it?'

'It's difficult to explain, here in the bar.'

'Then why don't you meet me outside?'

'T'ain't easy. Not now.'

'Why not?'

'Don't keep me answering questions. Go back to Greenwich, Bert. I'm no good to you. Not any more.'

She left him, hating it, to serve another customer. When she looked for him again he had vanished. All that night she was unutterably miserable. She didn't know what she wanted; she couldn't measure what she had lost.

Then, the following morning, with a beer-jug to be filled in his hand, Peter came into the bar. She scarcely recognised him. Sheathed uncomfortably in the tight jacket and trousers of a page boy, his hands constricted in white cotton gloves, he planted the jug on the counter.

'They told me you was here,' he said.

VIII

THE HAPPY ENDING THAT WASN'T

At Cambridge House a soirée was tailing to its end. In the Wedgwood blue drawing-room, ornamented with wedding-cake white reliefs, Lord Palmerston, wearing the water-blue ribbon of the Garter, was congratulating his wife as the carriages were called for the last of their guests.

About the state rooms, footmen snuffed the candles in the chandeliers. The butler was supervising the removal of the plate to the strong-room. There was a procession of staff carrying the debris of the supper party between the first floor and the kitchen quarters in the basement.

Under the critical eye of Evans, Peter was collecting dirty wine glasses on a wooden tray. 'After being lifted from the gutter,' a phrase which was thrown at him by somebody or another several times a day, he was expected, in the current concept of the rightness of things, to be living happily ever after. But once he had got over the surprise of being put into respectable clothes, eating regularly and sleeping in a clean bed; once the first novelty of his new surroundings had worn off, there was little to choose between the attic at Cambridge House he occupied with the scullery boys and the garret he had shared with Pa; not much difference, except that there was more of it, between washing-up in a mansion and washing-up in the 'Fortune of War.' Not that he expected anything better. What he had lost, creature of the streets that he was, was his liberty. He was cribbed in an atmosphere in which he could scarcely breathe.

Yet, when he tried to run away, it never occurred to anyone that he was other than ungrateful. Indeed, it was only at the express orders of Lord Palmerston himself that he was given a good hiding; and reinstated in the household. It was all done with the best of intentions. But Peter pined like a wild bird in a cage.

It was better now that Polly was at the 'Coach and Horses.' When he was sent out for beer from the servants' hall, he enjoyed the brief respites when she let him squeeze under the bar; and, on special occasions, took him upstairs to eat toffee-apples in her room. With the unpredictability that he had come to expect from people, he observed that Polly's attitude to him had changed. Now, she was always wanting to kiss him. And, sometimes, she had a disconcerting habit of wrapping her arms about him, and blubbing. He didn't really mind because she only did it when there was no one there to see them. But it didn't seem natural.

He had had so little in life that the rare moments when people gave him something of themselves bothered his understanding. He could contend more easily with the occasions when the rest of the world was taking it out of him. The soirées, for instance. He dreaded the soirées.

From the preliminary inspection of hands and ears until long after the last visitor had departed, the other servants, each of them exercising authority according to their order in the household hierarchy, never missed an opportunity of harrying him. As the lowest of them, he was the only one who had nobody to whom he could pass on the kicks.

That night, as he collected the glasses, and while the company—admirals and generals in the splendour of dress uniform, ambassadors encrusted with orders, statesmen in the sober black-and-white of tail clothes, women in whispering crinolines and proud tiaras—was melting into Piccadilly, Evans took it into his flour-dusted wig that he was idling. Bearing down on him from behind he soundly boxed him on the ears; setting the pace for future work by himself stowing a few glasses on the two-handled tray. Then he gave a lordly wave of dismissal. With his ears still ringing, Peter bent over the tray and lifted it off the mahogany table.

As soon as he took the weight, he realised that the distribution of the different-sized glasses was out of balance. But he didn't dare stop to rearrange them. Twisting his fists round the handles, until his knuckles showed white with the strain, he concentrated on conveying the load safely out of the dining-room; and Evans' presence.

In his anxiety, he took the wrong turning. Instead of carrying the tray into the reception hall and through a door leading into the subterranean vaults below, he blundered into the drawing-room where, seated in stiff Empire chairs, Lord Palmerston and his wife were discussing the events of the evening.

With a startled glance, Peter raised his head. As his concentration wavered, Palmerston himself half rose. The tray tipped off balance, the glasses colliding as they skidded out of control. In a wild attempt to recover himself, Peter made a forward rush. With a crash he deposited the trayful at the Prime Minister's feet.

*   *   *

As the glass exploded about his legs, Palmerston stumbled. Lady Palmerston gasped as dregs of wine from the fragments spattered the furniture and stained the floor. Bowls without stems, and stems without bowls, rolled in drunken confusion over the carpets. For one paralysed moment, Peter gazed at what he had done. Then, as horrified footmen closed in from other rooms, he dropped the empty tray, and fled.

Heedless of where he was going, scarcely daring to look, he burst open the tall doors of the drawing-room and plunged into the hall at the top of the grand staircase. Taking the curved flight two or three steps at a time, he hurled himself precipitately towards the marble-flagged entrance on the ground floor. When he was nearly there his legs ran away with him. Bouncing into the banisters, he rolled on to them and slid the rest of the way on the rail.

As he landed among the banks of flowers at the bottom, the last guests, waiting for their carriages to draw in, raised their eyebrows in mild surprise. But the fleeting figure passed through them so quickly that nobody moved; not even the linkmen at the front entrance. Puffing with importance, waving their arms, blowing their whistles, they were wrapped in the business of summoning the carriages, and intoning the proud names of their owners.

Peter ducked into the courtyard at a moment when one of the linkmen was imperiously signalling a brougham away. As the driver clicked his teeth and showed the horse the whip, he just had time to make a leap for the backspring. Hopping into reverse, he tucked himself across the bar. As the wheels began to twinkle, he stretched his arms to get a better leverage, and stuck out his legs to keep them off the ground.

The brougham, with a high-stepper in its shafts, swung

out of the yard before the astonished linkman could warn the driver. Squatting on the back, Peter hardly felt the nip of the short spikes—put there deliberately to discourage the attentions of boys like himself—pressing into his hands and rump. He stuck on, with the persistence of a blow-fly, until the carriage, moving down the slope of Piccadilly, was well clear of Cambridge House. He waited until the horse eased its gait behind a slow-moving nag in a hansom. Then, with a quick twist, he dropped on to the road.

The carriage was still moving fast enough to roll him head-over-heels; but, with the elasticity of his years, he climbed to his feet without mishap. When he was satisfied that he was free of pursuit, he crossed the street and headed into the maze of Mayfair.

As he hastened from one street lamp to the next one, moving into the centre of the road at the darker corners, he felt walled-in by leering, inquisitive eyes. He had worn the buttoned livery of a page long enough to know that he had cause for fear. As he cut through the back streets, where the Peelers wouldn't find him, he longed for the anonymity of his rags. The back of his neck tingled as, behind him, he heard footsteps.

When he hastened his pace, the footsteps hastened, too. He wanted to run; but, in the compulsion of fear, he couldn't. His arm was gently taken by a middle-aged man in a high-buttoned, long-skirted overcoat, with a crush hat on his head and a heavy cane, mounted with a billiard ball for a handle, in his fist.

'You're out late, laddie.'

His voice, which was educated, was thick and oily, and he had large blue eyes which stared like the jellies of a cod-fish.

'What are you doing on the streets at this hour? I expect you've been up to some prank, you young rascal, eh?'

He twisted Peter's ear.

'You haven't much to say for yourself, have you? Going anywhere? How about a bun and some ginger beer? You'd like that, wouldn't you?'

'I want to be left alone.'

'Nonsense. What you obviously need is someone to look after you. You're in trouble, ain't you?'

'T'ain't no business of yours.'

'Everybody can do with a friend when he's in trouble. If you're in serious trouble, maybe I could help you.'

The intruder raised the billiard ball on his cane to his chin, and gave what he intended to be interpreted as an understanding wink.

'On the other hand, I could, if I wanted to, hand you over to the proper authorities; and you know what happens to little boys who run away.'

'No, don't do that. Don't do that.'

'So my surmise is correct. You're running away. Never mind, you're quite safe with me. Let's have that bun and ginger beer; and there'll be plenty of time for you to tell me all about it.'

He wrapped an arm round Peter's shoulders. He was a big man, and carried his heavy cane with the purposeful air of someone who knew how to use it. He needed to. A man who ventured into the darker alleyways of vice took the safety of his life in his hands.

Half hypnotised, Peter went along with him. The man stopped at the entrance to an underground dive, distinguished by a lantern of coloured glass.

'Here's a place where we can have a nice talk without being disturbed.'

'Don't want to.'

'Why, you haven't even seen it?'

'I don't want to go there, I tell you.'

'Then where would you like to go?'

Now, there was a hint of asperity in his voice. Sensing his danger, Peter took the plunge.

'Can't I go to the "Coach and Horses," mister?'

'So you know that place. Well, if that's what you'd prefer, I can't see any objection. What a dear funny little lad you are.'

'I've been there before.'

Delighted that he had persuaded the boy to go somewhere willingly with him, he windmilled his cane in his fingers and whistled a tune to himself in satisfaction. With a buoyant stride, he walked Peter out of his life into Polly's arms.

As soon as they arrived at the 'Coach and Horses,' Peter pressed ahead. At a glance, Polly knew that something was amiss. Without uttering, she unlatched the catch of the flap under the counter. He was through it like a homing rabbit before his fish-eyed tormentor realised what was going on. When he did, his face flushed and his frame stiffened. He stood his ground, slowly flailing his stick in the air like a club.

Polly signalled Peter upstairs. She carefully shut the flap in the counter and, in a quiet voice, called to the landlord, who was serving in the adjoining bar. In the saloon, a little knot of customers, with an eye for trouble, took their glasses into what they hoped would be a neutral corner.

In a black rage, his fishy eyes narrowed into slits, the

intruder made a menacing advance. As the landlord peered
mildly round the partition to see what was happening, he
brought down his stick with a vibrating crash on the
counter.

'We know your sort,' said Polly evenly. 'You can get out
of here.'

Leisurely removing his cigar, the landlord called over his
shoulder to somebody at the other end of the pub.

'Fred,' he said. 'You're wanted in the saloon.'

A beef of a man, with the broken knuckles and flattened
nose of a prize-fighter, lumbered into the bar. Her duty
done, Polly gathered up her skirts to join Peter, while Fred
thoughtfully spat into his palms and stared pig-eyed at his
adversary across the counter.

'Are you goin' quietly?' he said slowly.

'I'll see you damned first. Where's that boy?'

He punctuated his words by thrashing his cane on the
counter. Fred glanced at the landlord for orders: the landlord gave a resigned nod. Stretching across the counter,
timing it exactly, Fred snatched the cane, and tossed it aside
as casually as if he were picking up a straw. Deprived of his
weapon, the trouble-maker looked away to see where it had
gone.

With surprising agility for his bulk, Fred took the opportunity to throw his leg on the counter and roll to the other
side. There was a quick exchange of punches; but the
amateur, powerful though he was, was no match for the
professional. Fred rocked him with a blow which spun him
reeling into the wall. Then he closed in and, balancing him
by grabbing hold of the lapels of his overcoat, packed in
four vicious jabs to his chin, nose and eyes.

It was all over in thirty seconds. Fred, with the practised

ease of a skilled chucker-out, spun his half-conscious opponent on his heels, ran him to the door and, with a parting kick, projected him into the outer darkness. He came back to throw the stick, with the billiard ball on the end of it, after him.

The landlord, thoughtfully polishing glasses, took charge of the bar until Polly returned. She seemed a long time gone.

When he heard her footsteps on the stairs again, the last of the late-night customers had shuffled off. All that was left of his cigar was a dusting of silver ash on the slopes of his waistcoat. Emptying his glass, he reflectively tugged his whiskers.

She was dressed to go out, with her shawl drawn about her shoulders and her pork-pie hat tipped over her nose.

'I've come to give you my notice, Mr Able.'

'What's wrong? Something to do with the boy?'

'I'm taking him away.'

'At this time of night? Why not think it over and wait till the morning? You're happy here, ain't you? Come on, don't be in such a hurry. Sit down and have a drink.'

'No, thank you, Mr Able. I don't think I will.'

'You're fond of that boy?'

He glanced over his shoulder as he refilled his own glass.

'Know who his father was?'

She shook her head.

'Well, never mind. Ask no questions, and you won't hear no lies. That's right, ain't it?'

Mr Able gave her a playful tap, and a knowing grin.

'You know, Polly, I've taken a great liking to you, even if the missus hasn't. You're the best barmaid in the old "Coach" for a long month of Sundays. Doesn't matter to me if you got your little troubles. We all slip sometimes.'

He reached out a podgy hand, unsuccessfully, to paw her.

'I'm sure I'm grateful to you, Mr Able . . .'

'Forget it. I'm a man of the world, ducks; that's me. Tom Able has seen it all; seen the whole, wide world in this very bar, I have. Same as you might. Get my meaning? You can have a good job at the "Coach," a 'appy 'ome from 'ome.'

'I've told you, Mr Able, I can't stay.'

So far as his face, which had the nature of an over-ripe plum, permitted a change of expression, Mr Able registered his disappointment. He prided himself on his ability, as a man of the world—and a publican at that—to deal with an awkward situation, if it wasn't too awkward, in a spirit of bonhomie and good cheer. Obviously, she was upset by the little bit of bother this evening; not that that was anything out of the ordinary. Chucking out difficult customers was one of the tribulations of the trade.

'He didn't do the boy any harm, did he?'

'No.'

'Then what are you narkin' about?'

'He's run away.'

'From Cambridge House? He's done it afore.'

'This time he's not going back no more. Not if I can help it.'

'All right. Where are you takin' him?'

She shrugged.

'Not back to Rosemary Lane where you was before? That's no place for a nice girl like you. What about that chap what's been in here? He's dead set on you, he is.'

'That's what he thinks now.'

As Mr Able stared at her enquiringly, she blurted out the rest.

'Even if I wanted to, I couldn't stay here not much longer; not the way I am.'

'So that's it.'

There was an air of finality in the emphasis with which Mr Able expressed himself. It was one thing to have a barmaid with a past who was pretty enough to bring in trade, and who might not be averse to the advances of a publican as well; it was quite another cup of tea to be saddled with a responsibility who would become a diminishing asset to the business, and whom he would certainly have to explain to a suspicious Mrs Able. As a man of the world, with a wisdom built on trite phrases and hidebound conventions, he knew where best interests lay. But he was not without kindness.

'Well, since you've made up your mind to clear out, I won't stand in your way. Here's a little something to wish you luck.'

He gave her half-a-crown from the till.

'I'm sorry I'm going, Mr Able. I'll miss it here.'

'Come back when you've put your little trouble behind you. Don't make a noise when you go. I'll tell Fred to let you out.'

The parting was unspoken. With a nod of dismissal, Mr Able watched her out of the bar. Then he sought out Fred.

'You'll be working with a new barmaid tomorrow,' he said. 'Polly's leaving. You can lock up when you've let her out.'

'The boy, too?'

'Yes, both of 'em. Don't look like that. They all have to go sometime.' As an afterthought he added: 'Know Angerstein's Wharf at Greenwich? If you don't you can find it.

When you've done your cellar-work in the morning, go to Angerstein's and find a bloke called Bert Hopkins. You know, you've seen him here. Tell him she's bolted with the boy. You can add that it's as sure as a bellows he'll find her round one of the pubs in Rosemary Lane. That's all.'

Having done his good deed for the night, and it was in truth a good deed because he had lost a good barmaid. Mr Able went to bed; and slept soundly.

Polly didn't waste any time. Humping her carpet bag, sharing a hair blanket with Peter, she crept out of the 'Coach and Horses' to join the rest of the fugitives and the homeless in the streets. Fred, lost for words, let out the two of them in an imploring silence. With her arm round Peter's shoulders, there was a moment while she hesitated aimlessly on the pavement. But the clatter of the door being locked and barred behind her stirred her to action. Furtively, she hurried him away.

Before daylight discovered them she was determined to put the greatest possible distance between Peter and Cambridge House. He had already discarded his revealing buttoned jacket. She believed, as he did, that some terrible retribution would overcome him if they failed to put everything out of the past out of their lives. Purposelessly, she was running away, in fear of the unknown, into the unknown.

They homed on the river. When he smelt it Peter raised his head out of the blanket like an otter over a familiar drain. Polly clung to it as if she too felt its magnetism. Never straying far from the banks, choosing the back streets, keeping a wary eye for patrolling constables, they headed downstream. Mr Able's guess was correct; not knowing where else to go to, Polly was drifting back into the squalor of the slums adjoining London Docks.

The people they passed on the way—night-soil men, road sweepers, street-cleaners, street-walkers—pursued their callings with only disinterested stares at the woman, dragging a bag, and the waif, bundled with her in a blanket, who plodded sore-footedly through the stale grey streets. They weren't much better off themselves.

In an odour of horse manure and soot, through the deserted warrens of the City, the two of them walked until they could go no further. Peter, in still unfamiliar boot-leather, suffered more than Polly. And, at last, his entreaties prevailed. She was satisfied that they were out of reach of pursuit. Searching for a corner, where there were no street-lights, she picked on a doorstep ringed by a group of amorous cats caterwauling over a dustbin. As the cats fled, she and Peter settled themselves on the unwelcoming stone. Wrenching off his boots, he immediately rolled over and buried his head in her billowing skirts. Tenderly, she drew the blanket over him. In no time he was asleep.

She tried to doze too; but she couldn't. Hot-eyed with weariness, brooding over the new life stirring within her and the child in her lap, she stared without hope into the night. If she had been alone she might have thrown herself, as Peter's mother had, into the chill embrace of the Thames.

The other time it had happened, it was only old Pa Smelley who had braved her into seeing it through; now, it seemed as though it was going to be Peter. But the brand was on her. She was a fallen woman. She took it for granted that, in her circumstances, Bert Hopkins wouldn't want any more of her. They usually didn't. Women in her predicament were an embarrassment. It was a man's world.

Distractedly, she dragged off her hat. The hairpins burst out of her fair hair and untidy wisps tumbled over her face. She didn't care. She stuffed her hat under the dustbin lid and abandoned herself, as she had before, to the streets.

When an inquisitive constable, patrolling the beat, turned his lantern on them, she spat at him as tempestuously as any alley cat. As he stood there, hands in belt and flexing his knees, solidly waiting for them to move on, she whined and swore with the facility of a harridan. In part, it was to deflect the Peeler's interest from Peter; but it was also that she had shed the remnants of her self-respect when she threw away the pork-pie hat with a feather.

Rubbing his eyes, Peter hung his boots round his neck on their laces. Polly covered him again with the blanket. Then, with a parting glare at the policeman, she picked up her bag, and the two of them got on their way. The Peeler watched them off his beat without curiosity. When they were gone, he produced his duty book and, sucking a pencil, recorded the description of two vagrants found causing an obstruction in what had otherwise been an uneventful night's patrol.

Now that he had got his feet out of his boots, now that the sweet stink of the river was filling his nostrils again, Peter's spirits were rising. Polly herself, as she identified familiar landmarks, felt less lonely. In a back street near the Tower, she took him to a coffee stall where the owner, a sleepy-eyed individual in a tall hat, smothered in a moth-eaten greatcoat and swathed up to the ears in a scarf, gave her a sullen grunt of recognition.

The stall was a two-wheeled spring barrow with a tarpaulin over the top and a clothes-horse, draped with a blanket, to keep out the wind on the weather side. At one end, two large cans stewed over charcoal fire-pots. At the other, illuminated with candles stuck in the necks of empty bottles, there was a display of gelatinous currant cake, ham sandwiches, bread-and-butter, eggs and watercress.

The two of them fed hungrily. At first, they had the stall to themselves; it was that brief interval between the night and a new day when the pulse of cities is at its lowest. But it wasn't long before dockers on their way to the wharves, harlots on their way to rest, seamen steadying themselves remorsefully after a debauch in Ratcliff Highway, straggled into the circle of light round the counter, putting down their pennies and halfpennies for mugs and half-mugs of stuff, adulterated with baked carrot, which passed for coffee.

At that hour, few of them lingered. Most emptied their mugs in a glum silence and, buttoning their coats against the cold wind, hurried away. Peter, with two doorsteps of bread under his belt, and something warm inside, slipped under Polly's arm and, promising to return, went down to the river like a child on holiday who can't wait to see the sea. Only she remained anchored to the stall.

'Ain't you got nowhere to go to?'

The coffee-stall keeper mumbled the familiar question—people must have been asked it tens of thousands of times in London every day—as he bowed over the tap of one of the tin urns.

'I'm looking for somewhere.'

'Got any money?'

'A bit. When that's gone, me and the boy'll get work.'

'The likes of you? Down here? Don't make me laugh.'

Nothing seemed more improbable than that the melan-

choly coffee-stall keeper even knew how to laugh; but
nothing was more certain than that what he said was the
fact. Polly knew too that, when the few shillings she had
were spent, it was laughable even to make a pretence at
hope. It was only the habit of past respectability that had
made her say what she had.

'I've seen you afore, ain't I?'

The enquiry was made without curiosity. As he washed
out the mugs, the coffee-stall keeper could have been talking
to himself.

'You was running along with the shore-finders, wasn't
you? Nastyface's lot. You might see 'em. They'll probably
stop here for a cuppa on the way back.'

In truth, the chance of encountering her old associates
again was what had drawn her, almost in spite of herself, to
the stall. She was ashamed to admit it, but, if she and Peter
had to live in the gutter, they might just as well run with
the aristocracy of it. The shore-finders—toshers in their own
vocabulary—were the élite in the scavengers of filth. Because
she knew how to add and subtract, she was useful to them
in dividing and trading the spoils they picked up in the mud
at low-tide and the loot, richer by far, that they brought
back from the sewers. Better that than slave in a refuse-
yard, peddle sprats on the streets, or scavenge for dog's
excrement and cigar ends. She waited for Nastyface, almost
eagerly.

She could smell him before she could see him. He exuded
a peculiar acrid aroma, which pervaded the air about him
like a burning dust-heap. He was wearing a long cloth apron,
with canvas trousers tied at the knees with string, and pads
of newspapers roped on his feet in lieu of shoes. A lantern,

which he had extinguished, was lashed on to his left breast. His mutilated face was half covered with a sacking hood.

Polly recoiled out of the candlelight at the sight and stink of him. She had forgotten that he was quite like that; that, when she had known him before, she was half blinded in a fog of gin. Although she believed that she had nerved herself for the encounter, she was afraid. She shrank into the shadows evasively as if, on the edge of disaster, she was running away. But the scarecrow of a man held some fateful fascination for her. As he put his penny on the counter, she hesitated.

'Done any good?'

The coffee-stall keeper put the question as he filled the mug.

'Three pennorth o' lead.'

'Ain't you been workin' the shores?'

'Tide's wrong for the shores. Been workin' the rubbish what they dumped in Goodman's Fields from that fire in Commercial Road. Anybody else whacked anything?'

'Nobody ain't been here; nobody 'cept an old friend, Nastyface. She's waitin' to see you now.'

The coffee-stall keeper nodded in Polly's direction. Nastyface stared, too, as she slowly moved into the light.

'So it's you.'

With a ghastly grimace of recognition, a distortion of a smile, he closed his hand on her wrist.

'Where you been? I reckoned you thought you was too good for us.'

Thrusting his face, which was noseless, into hers, he tightened his hold on her wrist to prevent her drawing away. When she turned her head, he twisted her chin so that she had to look him in the eyes.

'Come on, Pol,' he jeered. 'I won't bite you. I did you a bit o' good afore, and I'll do you a bit o' good again. You want to work for the gang, don't you? There's some good tosh waiting when the tide's right. The Old Un knows a place where there's a heap of stuff. He'll be glad to see you. Long Tom and Shifty too.'

She was doomed, and she knew it. She stopped trying to avoid the look of him. There was a dreadful pleasure in not wanting to try any more. But, when Peter came back, with innate prompting she put an arm round his shoulders.

'Who's he?'

'He ain't joining the gang.'

She said it without conviction.

'Is he yours?'

Letting her wrist drop, he lifted Peter away from her and planted him on the ground at his feet. He looked him over approvingly.

'Right size.'

'What are you talkin' of?'

'I said, "right size." I can use a boy like him for summat what I've got in m'mind. If it comes off I won't bash you same as I oughter. See?'

He turned on Peter.

'What's your name, tiddler?'

'I ain't no tiddler.'

'You mind your tongue, you young mudlark, or I'll give you what's what.'

'I ain't afeared of you.'

'Ain't you?'

There was quiet menace in his voice. Peter looked to Polly for support, but her own face was quite expressionless. She might have been a sleepwalker, incapable of independent thought or action. Peter sensed that she needed protection. On an impulse he ducked out of Nastyface's reach and hurled at him one of the tin mugs off the stall. The tin bounced off ineffectively as Polly, without protest, allowed Nastyface to lead her away. Keeping his distance, Peter followed them. The coffee-stall keeper knew better than to intervene.

IX

BURIED TREASURE

ONCE Polly had satisfied herself that Peter was following, he might not have existed. The strange hold that Nasty-face exerted over her was complete. Temporarily, it had obliterated her obsession for Peter. Not that he was put out. He trailed them doggedly, from one ramshackle lane to another, until they arrived at a public house which, even at that hour of early light, was open.

Nastyface had evidently discovered that Polly had some money. For a while, Peter hovered outside as they settled down to drink it. But he didn't dally long. The habit of self-sufficiency was too deeply ingrained. With a tuneless whistle, he forked his fingers in the lip of his trousers pockets and adventured back to the riverside.

It was low tide. The stairs to the water's edge were crowded with flocks of children who, if all their rags had been sewn together, wouldn't have produced enough clothing between them to cover any one of them. The shore was peopled with caricatures of humanity combing the mud for pickings with bent backs like gleaners working through a soured field. About the dock walls, a press of stevedores and seamen, carters and costers, merchants and shipping agents, toughs and idlers, enlivened the narrow streets of the wealthiest port of the world.

It was much more exciting than Greenwich. Ranging about like a questing spaniel, gazing at the cobweb of the sailing-ships' rigging, exchanging back-chat with the street traders, dancing on one leg round likely adversaries, cocking snooks at the dockyard guards with their muskets, raiding the barrows of the costermongers, Peter was as happy as a sparrow on a heap of fresh manure.

Sure-footedly, he made his way over river ooze where people could sink without trace—and sometimes did—in the quick-stuff, to collect bits of coal, lengths of rope and bones. He traded what he brought back for tuppence with a Jew. And, before late afternoon, he made another tuppence for quietening a hackney without its owner discovering that he had stuck a pin in its hindquarters to make a show. His life, which had come to a full stop in the stifling atmosphere of Cambridge House, was full again. He hadn't a care in the world.

He didn't even think about Polly; but Polly was searching on the bank for him. Maudlin with gin, glazed-eyed and unhappy, scarcely remembering what she wanted or what she had lost, she needed him again. When she found him— it wasn't difficult on the waterfront—she overwhelmed him with sentiment. He put up with it patiently; but he couldn't make out what she was babbling about.

They found a lodging. It was a hovel in which the broken panes in the windows were stuffed with old rags, where most of the furniture had been used long since for firewood and where the beds were two straw-filled palliasses laid against a wainscoting which rustled with rats. That night, Polly was too drunk, Peter too weary, to care.

They slept until early morning when he woke to find her holding the guttering flame of a rushlight over his face. She

was studying him intently, as if she had been doing it for a
long time.

'What's the matter, Pol?'

'We ain't got any money. It all went in the pub.'

'I got fourpence. That'll do to buy breakfast with.'

'We gotta have more money than that,' she muttered.
'What do you say, Peter, if someone I know puts us in the
way of a heap o' brass? Enough money for us to live on
like lords for months, perhaps longer?'

'What have we got to do to get it?'

She seemed to evade the question.

'It's much more tosh than you'd get for an old salmon.
You netted the salmon, didn't you? Well, Nastyface says
you oughter be able to do this job, too.'

'The chap what took you off to the pub?'

'He says you're the right size.'

'I heard him. Right size for what?'

'You ain't afeared of the sewers?'

'I ain't been inside them.'

'Nastyface says it ain't no different from working the
shores, except for the money you make. There's buried
treasure there, he says—think of that—treasure which the
grown men can't get, although they knows where it is,
because the old sewers are too small.'

Her voice grew hoarse with excitement.

'But not too small for you, Peter. Oh, I know I oughtn't
to be asking you—I know I oughtn't—but I promised
Nastyface I would . . . and you did net the salmon, didn't
you?'

She looked at him, the miserable rushlight dripping on her
hand, with furtive entreaty. It was what she had tried,
incoherently, to tell him the night before. It was what she

had been wanting to ask him ever since the gin had worked off and she had lain on her back waiting for him to stir.

'You don't have to go in alone. The gang'll be with you. There's golden sovereigns and silver spoons, a heap of copper and brass; and, maybe, jewels as well. When we whack it, we'll all go equal shares. We won't live in a place like this, we won't starve . . . we'll be rich, Peter, rich as mud.'

'Suppose the Peelers catches us?'

'They won't get Nastyface, not him. And they won't get you neither. You'll do the job in a tide; and, after that, you won't never have to go back in the sewers again.'

'I'm afeared, Pol.'

'Afeared of the sewers?'

'No, I ain't afeared of them. I'm only afeared the Johnnies'll send me to the House of Correction.'

She was ashamed of herself but, in her relief that she had enlisted him to help the toshers in their dirty work, it hardly seemed to matter whether he went to the House of Correction or not. It was easier to sacrifice Peter than to stand in the way of Nastyface. She eased her conscience with the thought that, in looking after themselves, the toshers would look after him. And, if the Peelers caught him in the sewers, he would probably only be sent away for fourteen days. She promised him that there was no danger even of that. Then the two of them went out to spend his fourpence.

In a conspiracy of wretchedness, in which Polly joined, the gang concealed from Peter the dangers of the operation; contenting themselves, and at the same time feeding their own avarice, by exciting him with stories of the gold they had seen glinting in congealed heaps of mixed metals.

There were three others, besides Peter, in Nastyface's

gang. None of them were known by their real names; they
had probably forgotten them themselves. There was Long
Tom, who was built like a drainpipe; the Old Un, who had
worked the sewers since he was a boy and, in his old age,
was as spare and fit as if he had spent his life in the country-
side; and Shifty, who had a sharp yellow beak like a blackbird and was as jerky in manner and voice as a blackbird.

As the days went by, while they waited for the right
weather and the right tide, the toshers grew more taciturn.
The stuff they picked up on the low water mark only
fetched enough from the Jew to keep them from actually
starving. Polly drew closer to her associates in misery.

Peter alone was unaffected. He lived for the moment and
accepted the unpredictability of the future as he had when
he went fishing with Pa. Most of the time he was kept busy
mudlarking for coal so that Polly and the gang could crouch
over a fire as they conferred mysteriously together. He was
carrying a crock of it back to the lodging on the afternoon
that Nastyface at last decided that the conditions were satis-
factory for that night.

As he trotted through the streets, a big man emerged from
a dockside pub who recognised him as he passed by. He
called, but Peter didn't hear. Hurrying after him the man
lost him, within sight of the hovel, in the maze of streets.
With his fingers tucked in his belt, he loitered inquisitively
in the neighbourhood, too formidable a figure to fear being
interfered with, too determined to go away. Bert Hopkins
had been looking for Polly for a long time.

The raid had been carefully planned. Polly had made
canvas trousers and foot-slops for Peter to wear. She had a
long apron for him, a hood, and a sack to hang on his back.

She lashed a lantern on his breast and, finally, she handed him a hoe. It was a pole of about eight feet long with a large iron hoe on the end of it. The rest of the gang were equipped in the same way.

Peter was delighted. With the hoe in his hand and the lantern on his chest, he felt grown-up too. When Polly snivelled it only made him feel more of a man than ever. The toshers slapped him heartily on the back and welcomed him to the brotherhood with a nip of rum, which made him choke, to warm his inside. Then, in the twilight of the afternoon, Nastyface threw a thumb to signal that it was time to move off.

The Old Un, Long Tom and Shifty stealthily followed Nastyface into the open. But Polly, as if she had a premonition, held Peter back. Falling on her knees, she folded him in her arms and kissed him passionately. It was only at his urgent protest that she let him go. He raced out of the lodgings, stumbling over the heavy hoe as he went, leaving her heaving hysterically on the floor.

When he got to the door, there was a moment when his spirits sank and he almost believed that the toshers had left him behind. But as he hesitated, wondering which way to go, he spotted them, standing in a little group in the shadows, waiting. He ran towards them, holding the unwieldy hoe with both hands.

The toshers, too, were in a hurry. Nastyface had spotted a stranger in the vicinity. He was right. The stranger had spotted them. As the gang made themselves scarce, Bert Hopkins kicked open the door of the lodging, and pushed his way in.

Leading the gang through back-streets and alleys, where the Peelers didn't go, Nastyface made for the river; the Old

Un carrying Peter's hoe because it was getting mixed up with his feet. On a flight of river stairs, which was too dilapidated for the normal traffic to use it, Nastyface whistled a signal. A low whistle came in answer.

A row-boat, with two men in it, squashed quietly into the landing-stage. It was one of the boats belonging to the dredgermen, who made a living scouring the bottom of the river with nets and hooks as the toshers hunted the sewers. Tonight, they were working together.

As the gang tumbled into the boat, they exchanged whispered greetings. Then, with two men at the long oars, they pulled against the tide towards Blackfriars. In wild excitement, Peter listened as they discussed the plan of attack.

Getting into the sewers at all had become a difficult feat because the Commissioners, to prevent flooding in the streets during the spring tides, had covered the outlets on the river with heavy iron flaps, hinged at the top, which only opened when the pressure from inside was strong enough to lift them and closed when the shoulder of the tide pressed against them. The device had made the illegal forays of the toshers, who regarded the flaps as a deliberate move to prevent them scavenging an honest living, more difficult; but, to men like Nastyface, not impossible. The spoils were rich enough to make the hazards worthwhile.

They made for a shore, downstream of Blackfriars, known to them as Cuckold's Point. When they reached it they lurked for a while, paddling water, off the bank. They waited until they were satisfied that they were unobserved and that the ebb had uncovered the sewer entrance. They timed it so that the keel of the boat ground into the sludge as the bow touched the side.

The wooden baulks of the river wall sweated with a green

mould which reeked of corruption. Lengths of iron chain, eroded and rusty, dangled over the toshers' heads with the dismal invitation of empty gibbets. At the bottom of an iron ladder, the sewer dribbled obscenely into the mud. No search for buried treasure ever started in a more noisome place.

Shifty was the first ashore. He stood in the bow to make a spring for the ladder as they lost way. The others waited until he had satisfied himself that nobody was showing among the warehouses on the pier. It was a necessary precaution; a reward of five pounds was offered to anyone who caught the toshers at their work. When Shifty was satisfied the rest of the gang dropped overboard into the shallow water. Unloading heavy crowbars they set to work to lift the flap over the sewer entrance. It didn't call for much leverage. The load of muck behind it burst through as they heaved. The sewer spewed about them as, inch by inch, they raised the flap until the gap was wide enough to crawl through.

When the first flush had drained from the passage, the Old Un, by virtue of his seniority, led the way. Peter followed him and, with difficulty, Long Tom after that. Shifty, relieved from sentry duty, came down the ladder while Nastyface conferred with the dredgermen who were to be waiting for them when they came back on the turn of the tide. Shifty unloaded a grappling-iron and a chain from the boat. Together, he and Nastyface heaved it into the entrance. Then they themselves clambered after it.

When they were all in, the dredgermen knocked away the shoring. The flap shut behind them with a reverberating clang.

*   *   *

Crouched in the egg-shaped passage, they paused to light the candles in the lanterns on their breasts, to divide the grappling-gear between them, and to gather themselves for the task ahead. Peter's heart was pounding; but, in the company of men, he tried to conceal his trepidation.

Nastyface led the way. Even the Old Un was bewildered as to where he was taking them. In the underground complex of London the map was being redrawn. The low level sewers, which were to carry the waste of the city roughly on the line of the Thames to outfalls in the lower reaches, weren't complete. Temporarily the new ones had been dammed and the old drains, emptying direct into the river, were still in service.

The gang dropped down, from one level to another, until they picked up the reversionary line into the new intercepting sewer.

'Not much hope o' finding any tosh here.'

The Old Un was right. The passage, gleaming with freshly-mortared brickwork, was as clean as a barracks. They walked through it, without having to shorten pace, or bend their backs.

'Time they've finished, there'll be nothing for us toshers at all.'

Shifty was right, too. But, while the new sewer was still under construction, it provided the toshers with a convenient short cut to the Fleet River. The Fleet, which had long been an open ditch of cess was now, more appropriately, a part of the main drainage system. But it still excreted sluggishly into the open river. Moving at right-angles to the unfinished low level sewer, it was the old cross-road flowing over the new.

To reach it, the gang clambered up a square shaft, just

wide enough for a man to pass through, with iron hand and footholds built into the cornering. They emerged in a clammy chamber where there was a penstock, a sort of lock-gate used to direct the sewage from one part of the system to another. Below them, glittering in the feeble light of their glims, erupting with odorous gases, they looked on the watercourse of the Fleet.

Nastyface reconnoitred it alone; measuring the depth with his hoe, sounding the bottom, noting the green mark of the high tide line on the walls. Only those who ventured into the sewers as cautiously as rats came out alive. The men who got trapped were not seen again until their maimed and broken bodies were hooked out of the river by the dredgermen or the police. During a heavy rainfall, the main sewers choked in a matter of minutes. Those unlucky enough to be caught in them had to scramble for the man-holes and gratings; or bolt up one of the branches with a high gradient where they could hive until the next tide.

The rest of the gang waited for Nastyface wordlessly, listening to the noise of water bubbling through a mess of drains, enveloped by the warm and faintly sweet stink of corruption. The empty city, under a city, had its own peculiar mystery; a place which even the most unimaginative of human beings can't enter without a sense of awe; a place where, paradoxically, the spectacle of the nature of man induces a kind of humbleness, the way pilgrims feel about themselves when they tread the aisles of a cathedral. For the toshers, half hopeful, wholly starved of grace, it was a time for silence because they lacked a prayer. Peter wriggled like an acolyte in church.

When Nastyface came back, he himself appeared, under his pointed sacking hood, like a monk of some strange

medieval order. He flashed his lantern to let the others know
that he was satisfied with the level of the tide. With a jingle
of chains they gathered the grapnel off the gratings,
shouldered their hoes and followed him up the bed of the
Fleet into the intestines of the city.

'Frightened, boy?'

The Old Un's voice, in the glistening underground
passage, sounded as if he were talking through a megaphone.
In the dark arched tunnel, where the dripping walls seemed
to be closing in on him, Peter's whole being was fluttering.
Down in the bowels of the earth, even the House of
Correction seemed less frightening. The Old Un, insensitive
though he appeared, understood. He put a hand on Peter's
shoulder.

'It's all right when you get used to it,' he reflected
reminiscently. 'Time was when I was sick every time I
worked the drains—not with the stink, mark you, that's
healthy, look at me—but the horror that was on me that
I'd never get out, never again. I gets it now sometimes, just
a little bit. It's worse where we're going in the branches.'

In his endeavours to help, the Old Un had only exaggerated Peter's fears. The deeper they drew through fungus-
lined passages, as complicated in their twists and turns and
intersections as the streets of London above, the more he
swayed with nightmarish anticipation. He plodded on
somehow, up to his groin in filth, with two of the gang in
front of him and two behind.

As they advanced, the men hunted the bottom of the
sewer with their hoes, leaning down to throw the light of
their lanterns over the river of waste. When they touched a
solid object, whether it was a bone or a scrap of metal, they
buried their arms in the muck to retrieve it and to store it

in the bags on their backs. Nastyface cursed them for wasting time on trifles; but they were ruled by long habit and perhaps by the need to direct their thoughts from the plan he had made for them.

'Where are we now?'

'Under Cheapside, I reckon.'

'Hist.'

Nastyface called them to order. They were moving under one of the gratings in the streets where inquisitive pedestrians could hear them. The Old Un closed the shade over Peter's lantern. The rest of them did the same. As they passed, Long Tom doubled up and ran his fingers through the sewer bottom. When coins rolled down from the streets, they usually settled edge-up in the chinks between the brickwork. He was lucky. He pulled out a shilling.

But, when he turned to show it to the others, Nastyface angrily dashed it out of his hand.

'You can pick up stuff like that on any tide. We ain't down here for pickings.'

With unwavering purpose and an uncanny sense of direction, he led them on. Peter could scarcely remember a time when he hadn't been immured in rotting walls, cut off from the air and the sky, skating through filth which froze his legs while the top half of him was sweating with exertion. He didn't know it, but he was breathing short for lack of oxygen. The others were little better off.

They stopped under another grating to take long breaths of what, after the atmosphere they had been through, passed for fresh air. They had been in the sewers little more than an hour, and they were within reach of a cache on the promise of which they had comforted their empty bellies for a fortnight.

The corroded lump had collected in a hole, where the brickwork had long since been eaten away, at the junction of two branches. The passage was little under four feet by three. It was so dilapidated that the wonder was that it had held together at all.

'Which of you was up here last?'

'It was me,' said Shifty uncomfortably.

'What was the air like?'

'Not bad. It was the brickwork what was the trouble. It comes down if you so much as breathes on it.'

'Never mind that. The boy's small enough to get through. It's the air what needs watching. Where's your candle, Shifty?'

With nervous twitches of his head and hands, Shifty removed the stump of candle from his lantern and, fixing it on the end of the hoe, held the naked flame inside the passage. The others watched it carefully. It continued to burn brightly; but, when Shifty dropped on his knees to push it in deeper, the hoe wavered and the iron head touched the wall of the sewer. The tap was sufficient to dislodge a stream of rubble which extinguished the light.

'See what I mean?'

Nastyface turned his own lantern on Peter.

'See what he means? You got to get in without touching nothing. You ain't got nothing to worry about. You're the right size.'

Peter nodded dumbly. He couldn't even see them. All he could see was the glow of their lanterns as they crowded about him like bats in the gloom. Shifty touched him on the arm.

'It's not far. You'll come to the junction about a chain's

length up the branch. The tosh, it feels all knobbly, is sticking out of a hole on the corner.'

He could hear the chains clanking as they drew it out behind the grapnel. The drain in which he was standing seemed like paradise compared with the noisome burrow that lay ahead. A notion seized him that he would never again escape from immeasurable tunnels or smothering smells. He guessed that this was what it must feel like at the bottom of the sea, or struggling for air like the man Peg Weekes had once told him of who was buried alive in his coffin. But, just as terrified boys had swarmed up chimneys, he too did as he was told. He hooked the grappling-iron over his shoulder and, retching, dragged the chains behind him into the unknown.

The sewer was relatively dry. He found it easier to get up it, pulling the chain behind him, on hands and knees. Nasty-face and the others, their voices echoing like gongs in a cave, egged him on. Measuring out the chain they were able to tell him how much further he had to go. Towards the end the weight was so heavy that he rolled on his back and pulled it, foot by foot, after him.

He thought he was going to be sick; but, when he heaved, nothing happened. There wasn't anything inside him to bring up. Giddily, he wriggled forward on his face. He almost plunged into a pit of sewage. It had settled at the junction of the two branches where Shifty had told him to feel for the lump of tosh. It wasn't difficult to find it. It stuck out like the top of an iceberg on the surface. Fumbling with the hooks of the grappling-iron, raising himself to throw the light of the lantern on what he was doing, he tremblingly set the arms into position.

Few boys could have done it; but Peter had shot a seine-net single-handed. Instinctively, he planted the points where they would hold. Then he was surprised to hear his own voice rolling hollowly through the sewer.

'Heave away.'

Almost disinterestedly, he watched the pressure tighten on the chain and the lump of metal, like a rotten tooth, shift in its bed. He leant back to let it pass. When it moved he crawled after it, increasing his own pace as the toshers pulled more enthusiastically on their prize.

In their triumph, the others seemed to have forgotten that he existed. With a hammer and cold chisel, Nastyface was breaking up the thing, a black truffle it had taken a generation to grow, into transportable pieces. As it splintered under his hand, the other toshers crowded round to assess the spoils. They weren't disappointed. Old gold coins, twisted lumps of silver, brass and copper, ornaments that must once have been beautiful, bristled like fossils in the broken bits.

As the gang loaded them into the bags on their backs, their excitement grew. The Old Un, after a lifetime's experience, conceded that he had never seen tosh like it before. Long Tom, who wasn't much given to talk, speculated on the feast he was going to eat of jellied eels. Shifty favoured pork hock.

'You can save yourselves,' said Nastyface grimly. 'We ain't finished yet. The Old Un knows a place—don't you, Old Un?—where there's a lump which makes this one look like nothing. We got three hours afore the tide turns. Let's make the most on it.'

'Ain't we done enough?'

'No, Shifty, we ain't. Let's make a killing while the going's good, same as we said we would.'

'It's dangerous, Nastyface.'

The Old Un wagged his head.

'Why don't we get out with the tosh while the luck's with us?'

'Yes,' Shifty echoed uncomfortably, 'why don't we stay with what we've got. We mightn't have it so good again.'

'What do you say, Long Tom?'

'I'd like to get out.'

'So that's what you all says; all of you except the boy. You're a fine lot, and no mistake. Haven't we planned it, haven't we waited for the tide, just so we can make a killing? And now you want to bolt, when the real pelf is just round the corner.'

'I ain't been there for ten years, Nastyface; and the rats was bad then.'

'That's not what you said back in the lodging. Back there, you said you'd seen the gold glinting in the tosh. You did, didn't you?'

'It's there all right,' said the Old Un uncertainly.

'Then what's come over all of you? We didn't come here to pick up shillings. We didn't reckon to get out with only a part of the tosh. We said we'd do a night's work that we'd be rich on. Didn't we?'

'S'right.'

'Then why are you hanging back? It ain't far we've got to go. There are enough of us to kill off the rats. And we've got the gear, and the boy, to get the tosh out. There might never be another chance. And, before you know it, you'll be starving again.'

'There's summat in what Nastyface says.'

'All the same, Shifty,' said the Old Un, 'I'm telling you it's dangerous.'

'Course it's dangerous,' said Nastyface. 'If it weren't, the other shoremen would have had it years ago. But we know what we're doing, don't we? We got this lot.'

'All right,' said Long Tom slowly. 'If Nastyface is game, I'm game.'

'What about you, Old Un?'

'I got to show you where the stuff is.'

'Shifty?'

'Me?' He seemed reluctant to answer. Then he blurted 'Suppose I'll go along with the rest of you.'

Nobody bothered to consult Peter.

They were venturing into a section of the old sewers which, at that time, it was beyond the capacity of the professional flushermen to service properly. Only the Old Un knew that way. With repeated warnings, he stumbled along at the head of them, feeling the ground at every step with his hoe. In places, they plunged up to their middles in holes where the rats had undermined the passages.

Until then, the rats hadn't bothered them. They were in sufficient strength to ensure that the animals kept their distance. But, as they pushed deeper into the tunnels, the rats grew bolder. Unaccustomed to the presence of human beings, they sat back on their haunches and, baring their yellow teeth, stood their ground. Soon, there was hardly a moment when one or other of the gang wasn't wielding his hoe to destroy one.

'If you gets caught in here,' said the Old Un encouragingly, 'you won't be seen again until they've picked your skeleton clean.'

'How much further do we have to go?'

Even Nastyface was feeling the strain.

'Not far in the way of distance,' said the Old Un, 'but, if

you wants to get where you're going to, you must take your time.'

The tunnel which they were probing was draped with tails of putrescence which could have been living plants or simply the sour sweat of a city's leavings. The Old Un warned them, however much their backs ached, not to touch the arch of brickwork overhead.

'It's dangerous.'

He mumbled the phrase again and again. But he knew where he was going. With the wary knowledge of a human rodent he found his way, after ten years, to the passage where he said the tosh was lying. A fall of bricks had half blocked it. It was plain that none of the men could get through. But the Old Un assured Nastyface that the treasure, far larger and richer than the one they had lifted already, lay just beyond the rubble. If Peter could squirm up to it, it was much nearer than the first.

Long Tom who, in the confined space, was folded up like a cut-throat razor, muttered in sympathy:

'Glad it's not me.'

Nastyface silenced him abruptly.

'You shut your trap. The boy's not afraid.'

Indeed, Peter was past being afraid. His wits were dulled, he dragged his legs without emotion, he didn't even bother to draw away from the rats. He listened to the toshers laying out the chain as a slave on a galley might wait for the coupling of the shackles. Nastyface had to shake him to awake him to work.

'You ain't tired?'

'No, I ain't tired. But I wish I was out of here.'

'You will be soon. All you got to do is to slip over that heap of rubble, and fix the irons again. We'll do the rest.

And afterwards, before you know what you're a-doing of, you'll be with Pol. You'll like that, won't you?'

Nastyface's manner had perceptibly changed. Never before had he talked to Peter in such warm terms. His own voice, normally so sinister and cold, was almost coaxing.

'Are you ready? Then off you go, boy. You're going to hook a fortune on the other side of that pile of bricks. A fortune, I tell you. We ain't been through all this for mouldies. It's gold from now on.'

Peter stared hypnotically into the noseless face underneath the hood. Like Polly, he came under the influence of it. With the stiffness of an automaton, he again put the grapnel over his shoulder and dragged it after him into the hole. But he didn't get far. He was too exhausted.

Nastyface, in the faint gleam of the lantern, realised what had happened and crawled in after him. The Old Un and Long Tom closed behind to lend a hand. Together, fighting for breath in the airless atmosphere, they dragged in the slack of the chain. Then Nastyface half lifted Peter over the fall of bricks. He slid into a pool of slime on the other side.

'Are you all right? Is the tosh there?'

There was an interval before Peter answered. Lying on his side, he used his two hands like a blind man feeling his way. The tosh was there. It was a mountain of stuff which must have been accumulating, not for a lifetime but for hundreds of years.

'Yes, it's here.'

'Have you got the irons?'

'Yes, I got the irons.'

'Can you see what you're doing in the lantern?'

'Yes, I can see.'

'Is there any gold showing?'

'Looks like it.'

'Enough to make us rich?'

'Can't tell in the dark.'

It was more difficult to grapple than the other one because it was so much bigger. But Peter struggled with the hooked arms, digging them into the pits of the conglomerate, trusting that he had done it right. Then he crawled a few yards further up the drain so that he could turn his light on the treasure as they hauled it out.

'Are you ready?'

'Yes, it ought to come now.'

He listened as they started to pull. Just as he had with Pa, he sensed the gang's excitement, and shared it, as they strained to bring in the catch. The mountain of tosh rocked. Fascinated, Peter watched it as it keeled over. It glittered in places, in the way that a pirate's hoard might have glittered after long interment in the earth.

He remembered hearing Nastyface say that they'd have to clear the fallen masonry to get it away. He saw a sinewy arm stretching through a gap to get a better hold on the chain. Once more, the heap trembled under the pressure; but, this time, the brickwork about it quaked too.

A few pieces dropped in warning. A deep crack developed overhead. Peter shouted, but it was already too late. Lazily, almost as if it was too aged to hurry, the passage caved in. It collapsed with a sullen roar which startled the rats for a mile about, and made Peter's ears ring with pain.

When he tried to move he discovered that he was trapped behind a lump of masonry which hung menacingly over his lap. All he could see of the toshers was a sinewy arm which still twitched weakly under the rubble.

X

THE TURN OF THE TIDE

A HALF-DROWNED cat couldn't have been more wretched than the poor creature who, hammering with both fists, clamoured on the inside of the flap over the drain at Cuckold's Point. When the waiting dredgermen eased it open, he slithered through on to the shore on his face with the sewage sluicing behind him. One of the dredgermen heaved him to his feet. He just stood, opening and closing his mouth, without uttering.

'Where's the rest o' them, Shifty?'

Shifty wearily shook his head.

'There ain't no more,' he said tonelessly. 'There ain't no more to come.'

'What happened?'

'Dunno. I'm telling you, I just dunno. One moment they was there; then there were a noise like thunder and summat hit me on the head. When I come to I was all alone, down there in the dark, with not a sound except the water going drip, drip, drip. Oh, it was horrible.'

'You're all right now. Where did you leave them?'

'Under Fig Tree Lane it were, off Holborn, where the Old Un said we'd find the tosh. You should have seen the rats, matey.'

He covered his eyes at the memory of an unspeakable experience.

'How long we got, Bill, afore low water?'

' 'Bout an hour.'

'That gives us four to spare. We'll need mattocks, I reckon; the crowbars, ropes and a hook. Are you sure you know the place, Shifty?'

'You're not going down there again? They're dead, I tell you, certain as cold meat. By now, the rats is gnawing them.'

'You pipe down. You've had a crack over the nut. There were a boy with them.'

'Polly's boy. I'll have to tell her, I will. What am I going to tell her? What am I going to say to Pol about Peter?'

Shifty was obviously concussed and he was shuddering from shock as well. When they got him into the boat, the dredgermen, with rough kindliness, threw a sea cape over him to keep him warm. Rowing strongly, they made for the Tower stairs.

It never occurred to them to call the police; the habit hadn't got round to them. But neither did it occur to them to leave the toshers to their fate. There was a comradeship in adversity.

While the dredgermen went to get the gear they needed, Shifty raced through the streets, as if he had a tin-can on his tail, to seek out Polly. He was in that state of half-delirium of people who, having survived a ghastly experience, look for relief in talking about it.

When he burst into the lodging, he was surprised to find his way barred by a stranger. Polly was standing meekly behind him.

'Well?' said Bert Hopkins. 'Where's the boy? We're waiting for him. Then I'm taking him and Polly away.'

'You won't. You won't never take him.'

'Why?'

' 'Cause he's in the sewer, that's the reason for why . . . he's down there for keeps . . . I'm telling you, mate. I saw him go, like he was a cockroach, under the rubble. I wouldn't tell a lie, would I, Pol? Not Shifty, not me what's been a tosher all m'born days.'

'Here, pull yourself together. You're not drunk, are you?'

In the candlelight, Bert Hopkins looked at him more closely.

'No, you're not drunk. Come on, man, explain yourself.'

'The dredgermen's going to try and get 'em out; but the rats, thousands of 'em, is at them already.

'Where are the dredgermen?'

'The boat's at Tower stairs. They'll tell you Shifty ain't telling a lie. They'll tell you.'

'I know him, Bert,' Polly whispered. 'Shifty's telling the truth. And I sent him there; I told Peter it was all right.'

'Never mind what you did; it's what we're going to do now. You'll come with me, Pol. I'm not leaving you here.' He turned to Shifty. 'You, too,' he added. 'I want to see these dredgermen.'

Polly obediently did as she was told. Shifty, performing a macabre dance in his hood and filthy apron, jack-in-a-boxed at the side of them. Bert Hopkins made grimly for the river. After jerking Polly to her senses, he hadn't expected this. The docker, with the drainy laugh and easy manner, had put up with enough. After a few muttered words with the dredgermen, they treated him as if a captain had been piped aboard.

The tide was turning. With the current flowing behind them, they made the return journey at good speed. The intention was to follow in the footsteps of the toshers up the Fleet, making an entrance under Blackfriars Bridge. But, with every pull of the oars, the dredgermen grew more apprehensive.

'Don't like the way the wind's veered, Bill.'

'No, looks like rain.'

Bill appealed to Bert Hopkins.

'Better give the Fleet drain a miss, guv. That way we might all get caught.'

'Can we get in from the street?'

'T'ain't usual.'

'What does Shifty say?'

'They're all cold, I tell you. Cold as charity.'

'You ain't got to do nothing,' Bert murmured. 'Just take us over the place in the street where you last saw 'em. Know that?'

'I oughter. I had a barrer once in the Lane, selling tuppence-a-pound plums, same price figs. But, s'welp me, I went back to toshing, and . . .'

'D'you know where you can get a barrer now?'

'There's a mint of 'em—empty ones—stuck where the costers keeps 'em off the Garden in the Strand.'

'We'll put you ashore to bone one. We'll be waiting for you on the stairs above the bridge.'

'You're wasting your time. They're cold.'

'If you don't hurry, you'll be cold, too.'

Miserable wretch that he was, shocked and exhausted, Shifty didn't demur. Floundering out of the boat, he darted into the night. Bert Hopkins supervised the unloading of the tackle.

To Shifty's credit he didn't keep them waiting long. They piled the stuff on the borrowed barrow and, following the

line of the Fleet River up Bridge Street, made through Shoe
Lane to Holborn Hill. Nobody remarked on them as they
trundled through the streets, or thought to question what
their business was. Any group of workmen, with a barrow-
ful of tools, can dig holes in the road without inviting inter-
ruption. When they themselves started to investigate the
manholes in the environs of Fig Tree Lane, it seemed to the
occasional passer-by the natural thing for them to be doing.
But even Shifty had never got into the sewers that way
before.

Fig Tree Lane wasn't indicated on the street maps; it was
too unimportant. Once upon a time, a fig tree may have grown
there. But, now, it rotted like the sewers underneath it.

At first Shifty couldn't find the manhole he believed that
he remembered when he was underground. When he identified it, or thought he had, it was obvious that it was going
to be a long job to force it open. It seemed unlikely that
the lid had been lifted in a generation. But, under a grating,
they found an ancient street drain large enough for a man
to drop through. With the lanterns, they picked up the oily
reflection of the water moving through the bottom of it.
Bert Hopkins took one of the crowbars from the barrow
and, spitting on his hands, burst open the cover. Then,
purposefully, he slipped off his jacket.

'You ain't going down there?'

'Somebody has to go.'

'You'll break a leg if you drop that far.'

'I'll use a rope. I'll try and get to them while the rest of
you is working on the manhole.'

'You mustn't do it, Bert. Not you.'

He brushed Polly aside, and addressed himself to the
dredgermen.

'When I get down, you can pass a glim. You'd better let me have one of those mattocks, too. When the manhole's open, bang it so that I can hear you. I'll shout back. All right, you can lower away the rope.'

None of them argued with him anymore. His manner didn't permit it.

He seated himself on the edge of the drain and, when the rope had been made fast on a street stanchion, he twisted his legs in it and, without hesitation, slid into the netherworld below. It was a drop of about twelve feet and, as he swayed down, he carried a fall of rubbish with him. But he reached the bottom safely.

'Are you all right?'

'Yes, you can haul in the rope.'

The others peered into the well of the drain as he shouted up to them, his face showing ghost white in the beams of their lanterns. The dredgermen let down another lantern and a mattock, Bert swung the light up and down the sewer.

'You want to work downstream,' Shifty prompted him hoarsely. 'The place ought to be off one of them branches to the left when you leaves the main drain. There's bad air there and, if you bounce your head on the brickwork, you're a gonner. Good luck, mate; and may the Lord help you.'

They watched him bend his broad back as he crawled out of sight. The dredgermen replaced the grating. Then, with fierce energy, they set to work to prise open the lid of the manhole. There was need for haste. It was beginning to rain.

With hunched shoulders, Bert Hopkins waded down the sewer with the shaft of the mattock stuck into his belt, waving the light enquiringly in front of him. When he came to the first branch, he crawled into it; but, almost at once, the candle flickered. He retreated, choking for air. In the next, the atmosphere wasn't so foul. He went through it on hands and knees and, as the sewer branched again, tried to keep a check on his bearings.

At intervals, he listened to his own voice sounding emptily in the tunnels.

'Is anybody there?'

There was no answer except a mocking echo.

He came to a dead end where, at the sight of him, a family of squealing rats plunged into the sewage. Backing away, he tried to puzzle his way into one of the main drains again. But he was lost. The passages crossed and re-crossed his path without any recognisable pattern. He was despairing when he heard a clash of metal in the distance. It was the dredger-men at work on the manhole.

Following the noise, as best he could through pipes where every sound played tricks, he got back into the main sewer. Wading against the flow, he searched for the point he had started from. It was mere chance that his foot was arrested by an obstruction lying like a trip-wire under the muck at the entrance to a branch. It was the end of the chain which the toshers were hauling on when the sewer collapsed on top of them.

He lifted it out to examine it. He gave it a pull. When it failed to move, he crouched on his knees and shone the light into the branch. He could see that it was blocked. Following the direction in which the chain led him, he was welcomed by the beady eyes of a rat peering through a crevice. Draw-ing his mattock, he hit out at it. A dozen gorged rats popped in panic from the rubble. Gripping the handle of the tool close to the head, he laid about them.

Then, lying on his face, he began to clear away the fall of masonry. It wasn't long before he uncovered the gnawed remains of a leg. Working until his arms ached, he hooked the rubbish behind him. Then, crawling into the main sewer, he raked clear what he had already shifted from the branch and, like a burrowing animal, started again. Bathed in sweat, soured with filth, he laboured on while, up above, the dredgermen still tugged unavailingly on the lid of the man-hole.

He uncovered enough of the broken and mangled bodies of the gang to identify all of them, except Peter. And, at last he pulled away a lump of masonry which exposed an empty space beyond. Reaching through the gap, he satisfied himself that he had penetrated to the open passage on the other side.

'Is anyone alive?'

He thought he heard a groan. Waving the light, he tried to point it through the chink.

'Is anyone there?'

A small voice answered him.

'I can't move.'

'Is it you, Peter?'

'Yes, it's Peter.'

'Are you hurt?'

'I'm trapped under the bricks. The glim's gone out, and the rats is after me. They've bitten me already. Get me out. I'm afraid.'

'I'll get you out.'

But he wasn't hopeful. To open up the passage he would have to move a ton of rubble and always at the risk that it would precipitate a further subsidence. The dead men were still more than half buried. He could only encourage Peter by talking to him, and letting him hear the noise as he worked. The dredgermen were slow in arriving.

But, at last, the signal came. Instead of the repeated tapping of metal on metal, the sewer sang with tremendous clangs, repeated three times as if someone was beating a Satanic gong.

'They've broken in through the manhole, Peter. There's more help on the way. We'll get you out soon.'

For a while, Bert listened. Then he heard the dredgermen hollering as they came into the sewer. He hollered back. As the voices drew nearer, he went into the main and flashed his light. At last, he saw lanterns flashing back. The dredgermen waded towards him.

'The men are all dead. The boy's alive; but he's trapped behind a fall of rubble.'

'Then we've got to get him out quick. The level's rising fast, what with the rain. We've got to get him out afore we're all swamped.'

One of them went to investigate.

'We'll have to leave the corpses to the rats.'

'It's the boy we've got to look to.'

'We'll never move the rubbish in time. The only hope is to get to him from the other side.'

'Can we?'

'Not if we wait to open another manhole, we can't.'

'What about a street drain?'

'It's a chance.'

Bert crawled into the branch again.

'Listen, Peter. We can't work through to you from this side. I'll find another way. You've got to stick it.'

'Be quick.'

'I'll be quick.'

The flush of water in the main sewer had already risen appreciably. The men pressed against it, Bert Hopkins leading, until their legs were swollen with the strain. At last they clambered on to the iron ladder at the bottom of the manhole, and scaled into the open air. Polly was too strained to speak. In answer to her mute enquiry, Bert Hopkins just nodded.

'He's alive?'

'Yes, but he's trapped. I've got to get into the sewer from the other side.'

Shifty, who was listening, shook his head.

'You'll never do it, not now.'

The rain swishing through the gutters was already giving fair warning.

'I'm going to try. He's off the third branch down the main. Where's the next main towards Holborn Hill?'

'You can go in at Leather Lane if you want to drown with him.'

'Show me where it is.'

Not only Shifty, but the dredgermen too, followed him with the barrow reluctantly.

'There you are.'

In the gutter, underneath a gas lamp, Shifty pointed at a grating. The rainwater was washing into it with an insistent bubbling popple. Bert Hopkins glanced at it recklessly.

'It's only a third full, and it's not as deep as the other. Give me the crowbar.'

The old iron frame yielded without a struggle. Bert laced the lantern on a bit of string round his neck. Then, dispensing with a rope, he dropped straight into the water. It was already waist-high. Spreading his arms, he again moved downstream into the sewer.

He had travelled only a few yards when he heard the dredgermen shouting on the street above. There was a splash behind him and, when he directed his lantern, Polly too was in the sewer, tearing off the last vestiges of her skirt.

'I'm coming too, Bert. I don't want to get out if you don't get out. And I don't want to get out without Peter.'

'You're in no condition . . .'

'Don't mind that. Don't mind anything. I'm coming with you, Bert. You've gotta take me—because I can't get back.'

What she said was only too true. He hadn't stopped to consider how he could get back himself.

'All right, keep a hand on my shoulder so I know where you are if you stumble. There's a bad bottom here.'

The rush of stormwater racing through the sewer was strong enough to force the two of them to lean against it to keep their balance. Holding the mattock in front of him, Bert Hopkins probed bottom at every step. If his calculations were correct, Peter was somewhere down a junction on the right. Tempting though it was to leave the main, he allowed the press of water to carry him on. It was rising steadily.

'Only a little way to go, Polly, and we'll get into the branches where it's drier.'

'I don't mind, Bert. But it makes you frightened, don't it?'

'Yes.'

'Where is he? Is he still all right, do you think?'

'Should be. I'll go first.'

He heaved himself out of the main drain into the higher level of the branch. Then he dragged Polly after him. Panting, the two of them huddled together in the mouth of the passage watching the flood passing them at right-angles. It was surprising that they had got through it at all.

'We'd better be going on. I'll give you a kiss, Pol, just in case . . .'

In the fetid drain, they embraced. Then, doubled in half, Bert made his way up the branch. There was a foot of water even there. But the crumbling condition of the passage reminded him of the one where Peter was lying. Raising his voice he called to him.

'Peter? Can you hear me?'

The passage called back his own words. But, moments later, he heard an answering cry.

'That's him.'

'Thank God.'

'It's somewhere to the right of this drain. Perhaps the next junction. If you value your life, Pol, don't touch the brickwork.'

Moving more slowly, feeling out the loose stuff, they crept on. When Bert called again, they could hear Peter's voice clearly.

'Shall I talk to him?' she said.

' 'Spect he'd be glad.'

'Peter, it's Pol. Peter, it's Pol. We'll be with you soon . . . soon.'

'Quickly, quickly.'

There was a dying note in his voice, but he was very near. When Bert Hopkins turned the lantern into the next branch, they could see him, crouched into the curve of the sewer wall.

Polly shrieked as a flurry of rats broke about them. Standing sentinel over Peter, the approach of the intruders had disturbed them. Flailing on both sides of him with the mattock, grabbing them in his hands, and dashing them against the wall, Bert Hopkins fought an army of them. In the candlelight, he flayed them with a cold fury.

Crowded between him and the heap of rubble the rats stood their ground, squealing and jumping at the light as if they were after his throat. But, soon, the dead and the wounded outnumbered the living. The survivors turned on the corpses of their own kind. With hands and arms dripping blood, Bert saw off the last of them. They were only just in time. Peter, too, had been bitten badly.

When they crouched over him, he seemed to be only semi-conscious. But, at the sight of Polly, he stirred.

'Where are the rats?'

'They've gone, Peter.'

'They nearly had me, Pol.'

A lump of brickwork, in which several courses were stuck together, had rolled across him, pinning him against the wall. But, surprisingly, he was otherwise unhurt. Bert wrapped his arms round the piece to gauge the weight.

'I think I can lift it, Pol, if you can pull him clear. You'll have to be sharp. It may bring down another fall with it.'

He curved his back into the opposite side of the sewer. When he was satisfied that the wall was holding, he bent and grabbed the piece in his fists.

'Catch hold of him under the shoulders. When I lift, drag him clear.'

As Bert took the strain, there was another sinister rumble as if the passage were crumbling again. But Bert lifted the limb clear. With a heave Polly skated Peter through the slush. Then, slowly, Bert lowered away the weight. As he did so, he could feel the sewer wall behind his back caving in. Using all his strength, he held it there.

'Get as far off as you can,' he shouted.

He held on, carrying the wall on his broad back, until the two of them were out of danger. Then, pressing his palms into the egg-shaped roof, he poised himself for a spring. The collapse of bricks as he broke away knocked him off his feet. But, somehow, he dodged death with a roll of his muscular shoulders and a dive of despair. He struggled out on his elbows, bleeding from a gash over his eye; but with only a trouser leg missing.

For all Polly and Peter knew, he had gone the way of the toshers. The fall had snuffed the candle in the lantern. Even Bert, dazed by the crash, bemused by the sooty darkness, had to make an effort to recall where he was, and why. It was only when he and Polly collided head to head in the tunnel that she knew that he was still alive and that he himself found himself again.

She ran enquiring fingers over his shoulders and head as if she needed to make sure it was him.

'Your face is sticky. Are you hurt?'

'Dunno. Is the boy safe?'

'He's all right. We both thought you was dead.'

'I wasn't too sure myself.'

'I don't like the dark, Bert. Can't you light the lantern?'

He fumbled at the crushed piece of ironwork round his neck; but the glass was shattered, and only the candle survived. That, too, was useless. The box of lucifers in his pocket was sopping wet.

'We'll have to keep close together, that's all. Just wait here while I try and recover the mattock. We might need it.'

Gingerly working up the branch again, he searched among the rubble at the length of his arm. When his hand closed over the shaft, he eased out the tool as carefully as if

he were dealing with a man-trap. The rubbish about it
grumbled as he pulled, but it settled without bringing down
another fall on top of it. Sticking the mattock into his belt,
he rejoined Polly.

'The sooner we're clear of this branch, the better. I'll go
first. You, Peter—are you there?—you keep hold of the
back of my belt. And you, Pol, you follow Peter.'

Passing to the front of them in the narrow drain was in
itself a nightmare. In the dark, they stumbled clumsily into
each other, dislodging more bricks in the effort.

'Get us out soon, Bert.'

'Depends on the level in the main. We might be down
here till the next tide.'

It had been fearful enough, in the scaly sweating passages,
with the guiding glimmer of a lantern. Now, they groped;
finding their way by touching the untouchable, guessing
direction by the gurgle of the water plunging through the
main sewers down to the river. Bert pushed his mattock in
front of him to feel out the junction; and almost lost it over
the brink.

They were crouching in a foot of water. What the depth
was in the main sewer they couldn't tell. But, reaching up
with the mattock, Bert discovered that there was still a few
feet of air space between the water level and the arch of the
drain.

'Can't tell if it's rising or falling,' he mumbled. Then he
lapsed into an indecisive silence.

It was a symptom of the claustrophobic horror that they
were experiencing that, as time went on, they talked less,
moved more slowly, and found it increasingly difficult to
concentrate their thoughts or regulate their actions. Bert
couldn't remember how long they'd been down there; he

couldn't read the face of his watch, even if the mechanism was still working. Polly and Peter grovelled close behind him, seeking warmth from each other's clammy bodies. To be warm and dry again seemed to be the only thing left that mattered.

'I can hear summat,' said Polly suddenly.

'Yes, that's a new noise.'

'T'ain't rats again, is it?'

'Don't sound like the squeals of ordinary rats. It's louder.'

Bert fumbled out the mattock and held it defensively in front of him. But what against he had no notion.

'You'd better draw back a bit, Pol, so my arms is free-er.'

'What do you think it is, Bert?'

'I wish I knew. But there's a lot of 'em; and they're working this way.'

'It ain't pigs, is it?' said Peter.

'Pigs?'

'The toshers said there were wild pigs down here what once tumbled in the sewers.'

'Had they ever seen 'em?'

'They said, if you sees 'em, you never comes alive out of the drains again.'

'He's right, Bert. The toshers say you only see the pigs when the level's rising in the sewer.'

'Then what are they doing down here? Why don't they never get out?'

'Nastyface said because, when the drains is flooding, the pigs always swims against the stream. They'll never get out. They're like us. They'll never get out again.'

'Steady, girl. We ain't finished yet. And we ain't seen no pigs yet.'

He pressed a hand comfortingly into hers; but there were

drips of cold sweat on his temples. It was no use denying it
any longer. Over the noise of running water, the sewer re-
sounded with squeals and grunts and liquid snorts. It was
the unmistakable chorus of a herd of pigs.

'You don't move, neither of you.'

But they were past movement. Stiff with dread and cold,
Peter and Polly clung to each other in their extremity, and
waited for the end. Bert, his fists clenched over the mattock,
strained for a gleam of visibility. But all he saw were the
diamond flashes conjured up by his own unseeing eyes.

The pigs, if they were indeed pigs of flesh and blood,
paddled by in a diabolical procession; clamorously, seemingly
endlessly and, for the three who heard them, with the fearful
inevitability of the voice of doom. With a burst of blind
courage, Bert Hopkins swung the mattock in the void. It
bounced ineffectively off empty sewage water. The race of
wild pigs, destined to root for all time in the waste of a city,
passed on.

'They've gone, Pol . . . if they was there.'

'We can't have just thought they was there.'

'We never saw 'em, did we? It's only if you sees 'em,
you said, you never comes out again.'

'What are we to do?'

'If pigs can get up the sewers—mind you, I'm not saying
they was pigs—we can get down. We can get out, even if
they can't. I'm going to try the depth. You can hold me,
Pol, in case I lose my footing.'

Swinging his legs over the main drain, grabbing her hand,
Bert slipped in. The pressure of water was too heavy, and he
was nearly carried away. But Polly hung on and he recovered his balance. Clutching the edge of the branch, the
level was just above his waist.

'Too deep for Peter.'

'Can't you carry him? We mustn't stay here.'

'All right, I'll take him. It's sink or swim.'

Almost sleepily, Peter crawled on to Bert's neck, twisting his legs round him, and leaning over his head. Bert stood his ground until Polly dropped into the water behind him. Without hope, they stumbled down the drain.

It was a forlorn venture from the start. In the heavy water, with Peter on his back, Bert reeled like a drunken man. He had had to leave the mattock behind; he couldn't manage both. Although the drain pushed him on, he didn't know where his next footstep was taking him. In spite of it, they travelled a surprising distance before, inescapably, he put his foot in a hole where the bottom had crumbled. He went down on his face.

Peter was tumbled into the current. By the time Bert recovered himself, the boy had already been carried out of his reach. He shouted, and tried to wade after him. But, in the velvet blackness, Peter was gone. It was all Bert could do to gather himself in time to seize Polly by the hair, and set her on her feet before she, too, drifted after him.

Polly, when she realised what had happened, gave a long-drawn-out wail. It was as much as he could manage to keep her from sinking into the flood.

'We have to go on. If we keeps going we might find him. He can swim, can't he?'

Wrapping his arm round her waist, he half carried her through the muck and the murk towards the river. There was a change in the pressure of water behind them, which made movement more easy. But it wasn't long before he noticed that the level in the sewer was perceptibly rising.

Vaguely, he remembered the tide. If the rising tide had

closed the flaps over the outlets into the river, the storm-water, piling up behind them, would fill the drains. He staggered on, as the level rose, without plan or purpose. He was near exhaustion himself; so near that, when he came to one of the flushing gates, placed at intervals in the drains, he rocked into the iron framework. Half stunned, he got through only to sway helplessly into the sewer wall, with Polly half drowned beside him. On the level of his chest there was a hollow. Exploring it with his hands, it seemed to offer an escape. Gathering himself, he heaved Polly into it. Then, with another effort, he dragged himself after her.

It was a blind ending, but it was a dry one. They were inside one of the niches, raised over the level of the drains, where the sewermen sheltered when they flushed the gates. He and Polly had to stick it out until the tide ebbed; but, when it ebbed and the drains emptied, he knew that he could get out with her through the Fleet.

What had happened to Peter he didn't dare to think.

He could swim. With the pressure of stormwater behind him, Peter was carried like a spent match down the drain. He was unbelievably tired. The wounds, where the rats had snapped at him, stung as the open places came into contact with the filthy water. He was stiff from hours of confinement in passages where he could scarcely breathe. But he had a will to live which was still irrepressible.

At first, he had no control in the rush of water; but, as the tide rose, and his head bobbed nearer the top of the sewer, he was able to feel the sides of it. And, suddenly, he found a place where the curved surface came to an end. Feeling about, as he had so often when he was searching for the mooring-rope of a barge, his fingers closed over a shelf. Getting a firmer grip, he wriggled on to it.

It was a platform at the bottom of a shaft, the sort of shaft through which he had followed the toshers. He could feel the iron footholds on the cornering. Dripping wet, he clambered up it. At the top, he came to another one. He shinned through it into a chamber under a manhole. He pushed on the manhole; but it was too heavy to move.

Descending the surface shaft again, he felt his way into a new passage where, at the extreme end, he thought he saw a faint light. He found himself under a dripping street grating; but it was out of his reach.

He was trapped as surely as he was when he lay under a lump of masonry at the bottom of the drains. But he didn't give up. Raising his voice, he shouted. Raking lumps of hard stuff out of the puddles at his feet, he threw them at the grating, and the street above.

XI

SIR JEREMY PRESENTS
HIS COMPLIMENTS

'STEADY, hoss!'

The driver of a green bow-fronted hansom see-sawed in his high seat as the grey gelding he was driving reared on its hind legs and jolted the elegant turn-out to an unexpected stop. The passenger inside raised the trap in the roof.

'What the devil's the matter with the brute?'

'Dunno, Sir Jeremy. Something's frighted him. Whoa, lad!'

With a flick of his whip, the driver tried to collect his animal. But the horse shied again. Stepping nervously backwards, sweating a little, he laid his ears and refused to go on.

'This would happen when I've got a confinement.'

Impatiently, the passenger pushed open the wing of the door in front of him. He was a square apoplectic individual with an aggressive beard, a bull neck and a big voice. His name, stamped on a pigskin bag on the seat beside him, proclaimed his profession. Sir Jeremy FitzHugh Smith, Bart., was M.D., F.R.C.P.

As soon as the horse was quiet he decanted himself into the road, grumbling into his beard and cursing the rain. Sir Jeremy, when he had a late night call, was seldom in the best of tempers.

'Must be something that's upsetting him. Is it a bit of paper?'

'He's usually steady enough.'

'Of course he's steady. Don't waste time telling me what I know already. See if he'll come if I take his head.'

'You can try.'

From his tone of voice, it was plain that the driver had little faith in his master's ability to handle the matter. He was right. After a few reluctant paces, the grey refused again. Sir Jeremy dragged on the bit energetically, but ineffectively.

'What's the matter with you, horse? On a God forsaken night like this as well. Not even a cab in sight. Get down and hold him, Dove. He won't move. Damn all horses, and all expectant mothers, too. Looks as if I shall have to walk.'

'Maybe I can handle him.'

'What makes you suppose that, if I can't move him, you can? From the way you talk sometimes, Dove, anybody would think that I don't know one end of a horse from another.'

'That's all right, Sir Jeremy.'

The driver, in a billycock hat and caped greatcoat, pushed him gently out of the way. He clearly had the measure of his explosive employer. Hissing gently to the horse, he soothed the animal while Sir Jeremy stumped up the road, seemingly warming his feet; in truth, letting off an excessive head of steam.

He had only gone a few yards when he shied himself. In the empty street, a clot of mud hit him sharply on the cheek.

'Dove! Did you throw that?'

'Throw what, Sir Jeremy?'

'A lump of muck hit me in the face.'

'There's nobody about.'

Dove continued his attendance on the horse.

'Somebody threw it.'

Hunting about, Sir Jeremy's attention was attracted to a drain in the road. He glanced down as another volley of wet gravel spattered against the rails. He was as surprised as the horse.

'Dove!'

'Yes, Sir Jeremy.'

'Come here. There's something going on in this drain. 'Pon my soul, I believe there's somebody down there, shouting. Bring one of those carriage lamps.'

Forbearingly, Dove did as he was told. Together, they twisted the lamp and peered into the drain.

'Can you see anything?'

'No; but, blow me down, there's somebody there all right. I can hear him. No wonder the grey refused.'

'What's going on round 'ere?'

Sir Jeremy straightened his back to find a Peeler rocking on his feet at his side.

'You've arrived just when you're needed, constable. There's somebody down this drain.'

In the dark, the Peeler gazed at him suspiciously.

'Are you all right?'

'Don't be impertinent, young man.'

'You did say there was somebody down the drain.'

'Listen for yourself.'

The constable, keeping a wary eye on Sir Jeremy, lowered his head. He didn't have to listen long.

'I believe you're right.'

'Of course I'm right. What did you think?'

'It's all highly unusual.'

'Of course it's unusual. It's unusual for one of my horses to shy in the road. It's unusual to find me here, staring down a drain, when I ought to be looking after my patient. She's probably had twins by this time.'

'Are you a doctor, sir?'

'What do you suppose I am?'

Dove nudged the worried constable understandingly.

'Well, what do you mean to do about it? You're the officer of the law.'

'I don't rightly know, sir. I haven't come across a situation like this afore.'

'Do you suppose I have?'

'No, sir.'

While his fiery-tempered master snapped at the bewildered Peeler, Dove was imperturbably assessing the situation.

'If I get a hoof-pick out of the boot,' he said quietly, 'we could lift that lid off. Then, if we lower a length of rope . . .'

'Have we got any rope?'

'Yes, I've got some rope . . . then we might get him out. Whoever's down there, sir, I think he's in bad trouble. It could be lucky that you're here.'

It was evident that there was an understanding between Sir Jeremy and his driver which transcended the normal relationship between master and man. Each of them, in his way, respected the other. Dove, more subtly than Sir Jeremy, knew how to handle his master. He knew, too, how to awaken the humanity in his heart.

'You can't do nothing,' said the Peeler heavily, 'what contravenes Queen's Regulations.'

In the presence of Sir Jeremy FitzHugh Smith, the policeman couldn't have expressed a more unfortunate opinion.

'I'll have you know, constable, that I am not concerned with regulations. I'm a doctor. What I'm concerned with is human life.'

'Shall I get the tack, Sir Jeremy?'

'Yes, Dove. How do you think he got down there, constable?'

'That's what I mean to find out.'

The Peeler cupped his hands to his mouth, and shouted through the grating.

'Who's there?'

'Doesn't answer. Yes, he does. I believe it's a child. And he sounds on the point of collapse. Is there a manhole we can force a way into?'

'Strictly against regulations.'

Sir Jeremy ignored the comment.

'He's probably had an accident. Never mind the drain, Dove. Let's look for a manhole. We should find one somewhere in the vicinity.'

Sweeping the pavement with the carriage lamp, mumbling with a different kind of impatience, he explored the road. But, when they found the manhole, they couldn't open it.

'You need a proper key for that,' said the Peeler complacently.

'Do you know where you can get one?'

'There'll be one at the station, like as not.'

'Then do something about it.'

'I'll have to report to the superintendent.'

'My compliments to the superintendent. Tell him that, in my opinion, the need is urgent.'

At the constable's obstructive stupidity, his exasperation was soaring again. Meanwhile, Dove was thoughtfully examining the grating.

'I must warn you,' added the constable heavily, 'that any attempt to force an entry into the drains, without official authority, is an offence.'

'I'll take full responsibility.'

'Then I'll have to trouble you for your name and address.'

With his notebook in his hand, the Peeler cleared his throat in the manner of one who has at last got everything under control. Sir Jeremy controlled himself with a generous pinch of snuff, closing the box with a snap like a pistol lock.

'My name is Jeremy FitzHugh—with a capital aitch—Smith. Sir Jeremy FitzHugh Smith of St Bride's Hospital.'

At last, red-faced but determined to preserve the dignity of his position, the Peeler proceeded on his way. Sir Jeremy saw him off with a jut of his beard.

'Feller doesn't even seem to know who I am,' he remarked contemptuously. 'Well, Dove?'

'I think I can get this grating off. Shall I go down on the rope?'

'Of course, of course. I will, too.'

'It'll be a tight fit for you, Sir Jeremy. I'll go first and find out what's going on.'

Taking off his caped coat and hard hat, removing his jacket as Bert Hopkins had earlier, he lifted the grating and made fast the rope. With no difficulty—Dove had the spare athletic figure of a horseman—he dropped into the sewer bottom.

'What can you see?'

'Nothing yet. I'll strike a light.'

Sir Jeremy watched the tiny spear of flame disappear into the passage. With his irascible temperament, it seemed an intolerable time before Dove answered him again.

'Where are you, Dove? Why don't you reply?'

'I'm here, sir. I've found him. You're right. It's a boy. Looks as if he's bad.'

'I'll come down.'

'We could haul him up on the rope.'

'No, don't move him. Could be dangerous. I'll look at him first.'

'It's not very wholesome down here,' said Dove doubtfully.

'What the devil do you expect it to be? I'll pass you the carriage lamp and my medical bag. After that, you can give me a hand.'

Sir Jeremy was no chicken. There was a lot of him and he was short of breath. But, without hesitation, he got out of his greatcoat, pocketed the stethoscope stored in the lid of his pot-hat and, leaving his clothes and starched cuffs in the hansom, followed his bag and the carriage lamp down the drain.

'Take it easy, sir. I'm waiting for you. Put your feet on my shoulders. That's the way. Easy now. You've nearly done it. There. Good for you, sir. Take a little time to get your wind back.'

'I'm all right, man. I'm all right. Stop treating me as if I were some sort of invalid.'

'The invalid's up the passage here.'

'Oh, yes. Of course.'

Dove held the carriage lamp as Sir Jeremy dropped on his knee at Peter's side. As he bent over his patient, his manner changed. Signalling Dove to bring the lamp closer, he gently checked Peter's pulse, raised his eyelids and settled his wooden stethoscope in his ear.

'Advanced prostration. Undernourished, probably starving.

Filthy, too; but that's not surprising. Is that blood on his legs? Yes, and on his arms as well. Multiple abrasions. What could the cause of that be?'

'Couldn't be rats?'

'Could be bites.'

'I've always heard they're bad down here.'

'I wonder how long he's been underground. Hold the lamp closer. I want to look at his conjunctiva again. No, not there, man. The whites of his eyes. Ah . . . I thought so. It's touch-and-go for him, I'm afraid. Give me the brandy flask out of the bag.'

He moistened Peter's lips with the spirit. When he stirred, he poured a teaspoonful out of the silver cup into his mouth. Peter began to cough. Sir Jeremy watched anxiously, waiting for him to open his eyes. When he did, Peter stared at them for a while without speaking.

'You're all right. You're in good hands. Don't talk now.'

'Where's Polly? You ain't Johnnies, are you?'

'No, we aren't Johnnies.'

'Don't let them get me.'

A look of indescribable fear passed over his face as, at that moment, they heard the metallic clanging above them as the police arrived to open the manhole. He twisted his head and seemed to make an effort to crawl away from them. But he was past it. When Sir Jeremy put a hand on his forehead to soothe him, Peter was sweating in the throes of a high fever.

The policemen—the constable had obviously returned with reinforcements—clambered into the drain noisily, talking to each other as they ducked through the passage towards the grating. Dove raised the lamp to show them the way.

'I'm the superintendent. Is that Sir Jeremy FitzHugh Smith?'

'Yes, it is.'

'One of my officers reported that you were here, sir. I thought I had better attend to the matter personally.'

'Your officer is a dunderhead.'

'He was only carrying out his duty, Sir Jeremy. If it was anybody but you, I should be compelled to take a more serious view of the matter.'

'It's serious enough already. This boy is very ill.'

'One of those toshers, I suppose. I thought we had got over that trouble. I shall have to take him into custody, I'm afraid.'

'You certainly won't. He's going to bed at once.'

'I must remind you, Sir Jeremy, that this is a police matter.'

'If you interfere, it'll be a matter for the Home Secretary.'

'Yes, Sir Jeremy.'

The superintendent was plainly better informed about Sir Jeremy than his constable.

'I'm going to keep him under my personal observation in hospital.'

'In that case, you accept responsibility.'

'Of course. Now, let's get him out. Move him gently. Why, what's the matter, boy?'

'You said you wouldn't let the Peelers get me.'

'They're not. You're going to hospital. Here, I'll take you myself.'

It wasn't difficult to lift him. Gathering him in his arms, Sir Jeremy carried him through the passage, with the superintendent and the constables following deferentially behind. If he had been a less distinguished doctor, if his personality had been any less forceful than it was, Peter would have followed Pa that night.

When he was handed up the manhole into the street, he was only half conscious, an object of pity to all of them who were grouped about him. Under Sir Jeremy's direction, they wrapped him in a horse blanket and laid him in the hansom.

'My compliments to Matron, Dove. Tell her to sponge him down, and give him a bowl of hot broth. I'll be along myself to see him later. And now, officer, I'll trouble you, if I may, for the use of your trap to go to another patient. We can only hope that she's as tardy as she usually is.'

Briskly brushing himself down, replacing his cuffs and stowing the stethoscope in the lid of his hat, Sir Jeremy, with a sense of professional duty well done, offered his snuff-box to the superintendent.

'You realise, Sir Jeremy, that I shall have to make a full report on this.'

'I shall be glad to see it.'

Utterly disarmed, the superintendent could only offer him a seat in his trap. When Sir Jeremy arrived at a house, with straw laid in the road to deaden the noise of traffic, he was still in plenty of time to deliver the baby. As he often said of himself, he was a lucky doctor. He had a gift of being there when he was needed. The terror of his hospital though he was, Sir Jeremy had hands that healed.

Five days later, when St Bride's was still mirthful with the story, by now greatly exaggerated, of the senior consultant's exploit, a party of medical students trooped after him through the public wards. Peter was in a bed, screened off in a corner.

'We'll take this case, gentlemen; a case which I have reason to suppose has occasioned some ill-informed gossip in the hostelries you frequent in the vicinity.'

Sir Jeremy stuck out his beard as if he were inviting denial. The young men avoided his gaze uneasily.

'Be that as it may, I shall be interested to learn your diagnosis.'

He threw back the screen as if he were raising a curtain on a stage. But, once he had satisfied his sense of drama, he patted the lump under the bedclothes.

'Hello, Peter,' he said quietly. 'I've brought some of my students to look at you. How are you? Still a high temperature, eh, Nurse? I thought so. Never mind, youngster. We're going to get you better. And you needn't worry about the Johnnies.'

Then he swung on the assembled students almost as if he were ashamed that they should see him off his guard.

'Very well, gentlemen. You know the circumstances of this case. Come on. You can't all have lost the gift of speech.'

Somebody mumbled, 'Yes, sir.'

'Now consider the signs. High temperature, even for a child of his age. Great prostration. Acute pain in musculature. Some vomiting. A little bleeding from lungs and nose. And I further commend to your study the colour of the conjunctiva. Well?'

'Could it be any of the exanthemata, sir?'

'Speak up, speak up. Of course it could. All the symptoms, save one, might indicate the onset of a variety of infections.'

'Typhoid fever?'

'Typhoid included. I commend you, gentlemen, to the exception.'

'Is there jaundice, sir?'

'Quite right, there is a sort of jaundice. Or there seems to be. But we all know, or I hope we do, that jaundice, with quite such severe symptoms, is most unusual in a child. This isn't the familiar jaundice; always mild in children, highly febrile, without prostration and without muscular pains. The only evidence of jaundice is the yellow tinge in the conjunctiva of the eyes.'

'It couldn't be yellow fever, could it, sir?'

'If the stegomyia mosquito occurred in this climate, it might well be. I could forgive anyone, even a qualified medical man, describing this as influenza, tonsillitis, acute rheumatic fever or, as one of you has suggested, typhoid.'

To the baffled students, Sir Jeremy seemed more reasonable, and forgiving, than he usually was. One of them gathered up his courage to ask a question.

'What is your opinion, sir?'

'I haven't got an opinion. Like you, gentlemen, I just don't know.'

It was an admission without precedent from Sir Jeremy in the history of St Bride's. He intended that it should be.

'I want to remind you that jaundice is a problem manifestation, a symptom of many ills of the flesh. It denotes simply a disturbance of the liver functions, or a partial or total arrest of the flow of bile into the upper intestines. It can be due to simple dietary indiscretions—too much cream, gentlemen—or to cancer of the liver, or anything. I am convinced that this is a disease, at present unknown to us, which infects, among other organs, the liver.

'Recollect that this child has been exposed to the filth of the river bank, has been attacked by rats and been entombed in the sewers. This is a dirt disease which derives, in some way, from the circumstances of millions of people dwelling in great cities, fouling its rivers, infecting its water. I beg you, gentlemen—when you qualify and if you qualify—to remember my remarks. That's all. I have an appointment.'

The students melted quietly away. The impression that Sir Jeremy had made on them that morning was, for most of them, to last.*

What Sir Jeremy refrained from telling them was that he knew no treatment for his patient except careful nursing and dieting. If the boy recovered—he thought it unlikely— he wouldn't know why. He was oppressed with a theory that, if London continued to grow, a terrible epidemic— something comparable to the Black Death—would decimate its population again. Peter's wasn't the first case of its kind that had bewildered him. Like many exhibitionists, Sir Jeremy, in his private mind, was introspective and uncertain. As he strode through the corridors of the hospital he gave a completely false impression of himself by inhaling a finger's length of snuff.

The superintendent of police had asked an appointment with him. In his consulting room, two others waited besides. Bert Hopkins, twisting his cap in his hands, and Polly, in new clothes, were sitting stiffly on hard chairs in the corner.

'I'm sorry to trouble you, Sir Jeremy, but these are the two people I reported to you about. They know the boy.'

'Is he all right?'

Polly half rose from her seat.

'I wish I could tell you that he is. I understand from the

---

* Sir Jeremy's anticipation of a specific clinical and pathological entity was described by Weil and Matthieu in 1886; its cause by the invention of the dark ground microscope and the discovery of the spirochaele by the Japanese Juada in 1914. Leptospirosis is a disease passed into water by the urine of rats, and occasionally dogs. To this day, mild cases are sometimes identified as influenza!

police that you two penetrated the sewers in an attempt to rescue him. Have you subsequently had any illness?'

'Not that I know of,' said Bert.

'No shivering, headaches, muscular pains, internal disorders? No? Pity. What about her?'

'I'm all right.'

'Married?'

'We mean to be—don't we, Bert?—quite soon.'

'Not too soon, by the look of things.'

Sir Jeremy planted himself at his desk.

'I have your report here, Superintendent. Did this man, Shifty, you questioned, show any symptoms of fever or haemorrhage? Or the boatmen?'

'No, sir.'

'I thought it right,' Bert Hopkins interrupted, 'to go to the police—for everybody's sake. Besides, we didn't know what had happened to Peter.'

'I'm not interested in police—or personal—matters. I'm a doctor.'

'Can't you tell us about Peter?'

'He's alive. What I can't understand is why you're not all as ill as he is.'

He glanced at the superintendent.

'This doesn't advance us any further.'

'I'm sorry, sir. Is there anything else? I've been instructed by the Home Office to give you any help I can.'

'I thought I might learn something; I haven't.'

'This couple, who have been of the greatest help to the police, are anxious to see the boy.'

'It might help; I can't. Tell me, what's the truth of this story that the boy was a page in Lord Palmerston's household?'

Polly reddened.

'He didn't do no wrong, sir.'

Sir Jeremy stared at her inquisitively.

'Honest, he didn't. We're poor folk, we are. We ran away because we had to. The Johnnies was after us.'

'We've got a check on that,' said the superintendent officiously. 'One of our men moved them on in the city. Described them as vagrants. They were heading, as events turned out, to the Dock area.'

Sir Jeremy tapped his foot impatiently on the floor.

'None of this helps me to treat the child.'

'I'm sure I could help if I saw him,' said Polly imploringly.

'Very well; you certainly can't do less, and you might very well be able to help him more than I can. Nurse!'

A head nurse, in a dark serge dress with a starched white apron, came into the room. Sir Jeremy indicated Bert and Polly with what might have been interpreted as a rude jab of his quill pen.

'Let them see the child, whatever the number is, in the St Mary's ward.'

Polly and Bert departed without a nod from him. Sir Jeremy had only a perfunctory handshake for the police superintendent. But, when they had all gone, he selected a wafer from the rack on his desk.

'Sir Jeremy FitzHugh Smith, Bart.,' he wrote, 'presents his compliments to the Prime Minister, and requests the courtesy of an interview at Lord Palmerston's convenience.'

He dusted the wet ink with sand as if he were arguing with Dove.

XII

A GLIMPSE OF ARCADIA

SIR JEREMY'S recommendation to the Prime Minister that a special committee should be set up to examine the dangers to national health of polluted rivers; his peremptory request for immediate legislation to control the activities of human scavengers between the high and low water marks of the Thames; his dark prediction that, unless something was done to check the growth of London's population, he couldn't as a medical man, answer for the consequences, had little effect.

Lord Palmerston blandly reminded him that a Royal Commission had already been sitting for many months, taking expert evidence on the state of the salmon fisheries with special regard, *inter alia*, to the decline of the fish in certain polluted rivers, including the Thames. He pointed out that, when the new intercepting sewers were completed, the experts didn't doubt that the more noisome aspects of the Thames in recent years would be relieved. He ventured to remark that, if the shore-finders and the mudlarks were interfered with in their admittedly lowly occupations, it might be regarded as an unwarrantable intrusion upon the rights and liberties of the subject.

He seemed more concerned to learn what new treatment Sir Jeremy had to suggest for the amelioration of his gout.

Slyly, he implied that doctors should leave politicians to their own business, and that politicians looked to doctors to mind theirs. Although Sir Jeremy huffed and blowed, it was to no purpose; except for the consequence that it had for a patient he had given up for dead.

Peter was getting better. Slowly, after weeks on the danger list, warmth and rest and regular nourishment were helping him towards recovery. Sir Jeremy couldn't but exult at his success. The Prime Minister, on the professional visits of his medical adviser, never failed to enquire how the boy, who caught the salmon and dropped the tray, was getting on. Each of them had reason to be interested in him. For Sir Jeremy, he had become the protagonist of a cause. For Palmerston, he was a pin that he had pricked into the swollen pomposity of his Chancellor. He still didn't like Gladstone.

When the time came when Sir Jeremy decided that Peter was well enough to leave hospital, he summoned Bert Hopkins and Polly into his consulting room. He confided to them a plan for the boy's convalescence. What he didn't mention was who it was who had conceived it.

So it happened that, on a butterfly day in early summer, Mr and Mrs Bert Hopkins, with Peg Weekes in attendance, shyly escorted Peter into the throng of travellers on Waterloo Bridge Station. They were in plenty of time. The South Western's Express wasn't due to leave for another half an hour.

Bert, in a clean white choker, bought a third-class half-single ticket to Bishop's Stoke. Polly, in a new dress and a new shawl—she had to wait for a while before she regained a figure to show off her new crinoline—obtained a tea-basket. Peg Weekes—himself an object of interest, in his old uniform, to the travellers of a new age—just stared.

For Polly, the nightmare was over. For Peg Weekes, it was an exciting day out. But only the joint efforts of the three of them had got Peter to the station.

The promise that he wasn't to be shut up in another mansion, an institution, or a House of Correction—or that he wouldn't get another hiding wherever he went—only partly reassured him. He couldn't understand why Sir Jeremy wouldn't let him go back to Greenwich with Polly and Bert. Even weeks of kindness in the hospital hadn't rid him of the deep dread that there was a catch in it somewhere. When he was told that he was going for a ride on the railway, he was sure.

Of them all, it had to be Peg Weekes to persuade him to face that. Peg told him, without a notion what he was talking about that, if he stowed aboard a train, he would go to a place where Peelers didn't exist. He undertook to come personally to the station to see that 'them swell Cockneys' didn't make any trouble. At the time, Peter believed him. But now, wriggling uncomfortably in stiff clean clothes, surrounded by new sights, enveloped in smoky smells, he wasn't so certain. Only Polly's watchful eye, and the comforting shambling presence of Peg himself, prevented him from cut-and-running again.

He was to be placed under the care of the guard. The guard, an official in a peaked cap and neckerchief with a long coat, a proper sense of his own importance, and a double row of six brass buttons to emphasise it, showed them a seat in a compartment adjoining the luggage van. He supervised the loading of Peter's new wooden trunk and then, when he was asked—with suitable deference—whether there was time to look at the engine, consulted his turnip watch and granted the request. For all of them, as they trooped up the platform, it was a memorable moment.

Lord Palmerston himself hadn't got over his wonder that, with the coming of the railways, he could have luncheon in London and arrive at his country seat in time for dinner in the evening. Bert and Polly, Peg Weekes and Peter, stared open-mouthed at the hissing locomotive. With the disinterested air of those who are accustomed to, and like, being looked at, the driver showed off his head of steam, and the fireman casually oiled the works.

The three o'clock Express to Southampton, which did the run in little more than two hours, with stops, made a brave show. For Peter it had an awful fascination like stealing a look at a picture in a forbidden book. He turned appealingly to Peg, but the old man had no eyes except for the gleaming pistons and the glittering brasswork of the engine. At last, Peter dragged on Polly's arm.

'Let's go from here.'

'Why, don't you like the engine?'

'Why must I be sent to the country, Pol?'

'You heard what Sir Jeremy said; it's for your own good. You ain't still afeared of the train, are you?'

Peter shook his head; but it was without conviction.

'Why can't I come back to Greenwich with you?'

'Because Sir Jeremy says you can't; not till you're well again.'

'When's that going to be?'

The question was never answered. The porters were shouting, 'All aboard.' When they hustled him down the platform, the guard was waiting outside the compartment with a key. There was no time for good-byes. Bert lifted him into the empty carriage. With a decisive twist, the guard locked the door behind him. Peter pressed his nose against the grimy carriage window while Polly flapped her hand at him through the glass. He had a last glimpse of Peg Weekes and Bert looking up and down the platform as the guard blew his whistle, flagging away the train. Then, in a cloud of steam, they passed out of his ken.

He didn't weep. He made himself as small as possible in a corner of the oblong compartment and, too petrified to move, listened to the rhythmic clatter of the wheels on the line as the train gathered speed.

To people who had never travelled faster than fifteen miles an hour, the train seemed so swift that passengers had the impression that they were flying through the air. As a consequence, there were many who were afraid to travel in the trains at all. In two hours, in the bare compartment, Peter re-lived the waking terrors of his own life.

The clank of the wheels made a noise in his ears like the clank of the toshers' chain. The tunnels, as the train nosed into them, made him retch as if he were back in the drains. As the landscape streamed past, he saw it with the same blurred vision as the night when he fled down the stairs at Cambridge House and the day when he ran off with the salmon from the fishmonger's slab. The swaying motion of the train made his head reel, the way it had when he was sinking under the corks of Pa's net.

When the guard came to unlock the door, and see him off the train at Bishop's Stoke, he found him slumped across the seat. On trembling legs, he had to be helped into the wagon which had been sent to collect him.

It was another week before the fever subsided; and he

awoke one morning to gaze abstractedly at an arm of foliage, heavy with roses, which was nodding at him through an open window. Beyond, the house-martins were carving the air for insects. He discovered himself listening to the orchestra of innumerable birds.

'Where am I?'

A plump red-faced woman, in a print dress, with a business-like apron, had come into the bedroom. She raised her hands in pleased surprise.

'So you've stopped talking nonsense at last. Why, bless my heart, I was starting to think there was no end to it.'

She spoke with a rich Hampshire accent. Bustling about the room, she tucked him up in the bedclothes and rested her hand on his head. As she waited to satisfy herself that the fever had abated, she looked out of the window.

'Those blooming old roses just won't stay where you nail them on the wall. Jack'll have to get his ladder to them. But they're pretty, aren't they?'

Peter smiled under her hand.

'Why, I truly believe you're better. And Sir Jeremy thought we'd got another tenant for the graveyard.'

'Sir Jeremy?'

'His Lordship brought him down special to see you.'

'His Lordship?'

'How silly of me; of course you didn't know. You've been very ill, Peter. When you came here, I was worried myself. But, as I always say, a little bit of country air can work more wonders than all them doctors put together. Not that Sir Jeremy isn't a very clever man. His Lordship won't have a word said against him. Her Ladyship, too.'

'You still ain't told me where I am? I ain't been here afore. I knows that.'

'Why, bless you, this is Broadlands. Lord Palmerston's.'
'T'ain't a mansion, is it?'

'What are you worrying about? Of course it isn't a mansion. I never heard such a thing. This is the cottage where Jack and me live. His Lordship is in the big house. Her Ladyship has been to see you, did you know that? And me with m'dirty old apron on. My, she looked beautiful. The biggest crinoline I've ever set my born eyes on. She'll be pleased we're getting you better. Now, what about a nice boiled egg for breakfast? You haven't been eating anything at all. And, as I say to Jack, I like to see a man eat. You'll want a cup of tea, too; and I've got some new bread, just baked, and the best lot of butter I've churned in weeks. You can taste the buttercups in it.'

Peter didn't understand a half of what she was gossiping about. But he experienced a glow of kindness which he had never known before. Polly had never talked to him like that. When she left the room, he lay on his back and watched the clouds drifting across the blue aquatinted sky. He felt unbelievably peaceful.

Mr and Mrs Jack Cragg filled his new life. Jack, who was the water bailiff of the Palmerston estate, was never tired of getting him to tell the story of how he netted the Thames salmon. He promised Peter that, when he was well, they would together catch a salmon again. But he couldn't convince him.

When Peter looked out from his bedroom window on to the silver ribbon of the Test, winding through the broad valley down to the sea at Southampton, he wasn't impressed. The stream wasn't big enough to float a penny steamer. Jack Cragg laughed.

'This is a big river, son,' he said.

He might have been Pa talking.

'They go thirty, forty pounds in the spring run. This time of year, twenty pounds is nothing. You'll see.'

There came a day, when the spent mayflies drifted down the stream like broken galleons, a day when the surface of the river was white with crowsfoot, and the banks were decked in yellow flags, when Jack Cragg took him to the bank. He brought a great rod of hickory, sixteen feet long, and his reel with its line of horsehair and silk. The ribbon of his hard hat was decked with gaily-coloured flies.

They crossed the river over a line of baulks, used to set the nets when they were weed-cutting, on to the lawns of Broadlands House; 'a seat,' as Lord Palmerston himself had said, 'fit for a gentleman.' It was.

The huge square mansion sat comfortably overlooking the river, ringed with its topiary garden, its goldfish pond, its orangery, its shrubberies, and the annexe Palmerston had added at the side. Jack Cragg turned away from the house. He led Peter down a gravel path, with a copse at the side of it, along the banks of the river.

A trout rose to a mayfly as it passed over his dining-room. A water vole, swimming to his holt, stopped on the bank to look them over inquisitively. A pair of swans, raising their wings and straightening their necks in challenge, hissed at them as they went by. A mallard drake, in the eclipse of his plumage, flapped away over the surface of the water. It was the Rookery Beat and, in the clamour of a rookery, Jack Cragg tied on a fly and worked it through the water.

Nobody had believed that Peter had netted a salmon in the Thames. Nobody who didn't know could suppose that there were salmon in the lower reaches of the Test. It was so small a river. But, as Jack Cragg worked his fly over the likely lies, there was a swirl in the water.

'He's there,' Peter shouted. 'He's there. He's lying off the bank. Our Father what art in Heaven . . .'

Jack smiled. Changing the angle of his cast, he offered the fly again. The fish took him with a heavy double-pull. Lifting his rod-point, the hook went home.

'Here you are, Peter. He's yours.'

He passed the rod to him.

'He'll lie quiet until you give him the butt. Control the line with your finger, there. When he runs, let him have it. When he stops, gain every yard on the reel you can. Don't let him get downstream of you. Gently, now.'

Peter never noticed the weight of the rod. With an inherited skill, he played the fish as if he had been doing it all his life. It was only occasionally that Jack had to tell him to correct the angle of his point. to remind him that the fish had got plenty of fight in him yet, to tell him to change his position on the bank.

After his first excited exclamation, Peter himself never spoke. He was lost in an experience which effaced everything that had gone before. From that moment, when he felt the fish shaking his head, lashing his spade tail, at the end of the rod, he found himself. When Jack Cragg tailed the exhausted salmon out of the water, Peter threw his arms about it, and kissed its silver flank. His heart was too full to notice two newcomers.

'Thank you, Jack.'

With Lady Palmerston on his arm, the Prime Minister joined them on the bank. By arrangement, he had been watching them from a thatched hut overlooking the river.

'Good afternoon, m'lord.'

'I think we have the makings of a future river keeper here.'

'I think so.'

At the sound of the voices, Peter looked up from the fish. When he saw Lord Palmerston, he nearly ran away again. But the old eyes were smiling.

'It's all right, boy. You're no page but, by heaven, you played that salmon like a fisherman. Cragg here thinks he can make something of you. Would you like to stay with us at Broadlands?'

Peter could only swallow the frog in his throat.

He never went back to Greenwich, except once, years later, for Peg Weekes' funeral. But Polly and Bert, first with one baby and then more, came from London to see him. They treated him with a respect commensurate with his new status.

In his lifetime, Peter became a legend. The boy who caught the last salmon in London's River is the man who is still talked about today, in little inns where anglers meet, as 'the wizard of the Test.' It is perhaps irrelevant to this story that, at the present time, his grandson is one of the best known river keepers in the chalk-stream country.

An Historical Note on
The Passing of the Thames Salmon

It is a fragment of history that, on March 21st, 1861, Big Ben startled Londoners by chiming twenty times at three o'clock in the morning. It is also correct, according to a computation kindly made for me by the Director of Liverpool Observatory, that on that night at the same hour the tide started to flow in Greenwich Reach. Whether that was the tide on which the last of the now vanished race of Thames salmon ran up the river is a matter of faith; like the story that, at one time, salmon were so prolific in the Thames that London apprentices used to have a clause in their indentures stipulating that they weren't to be fed on the fish more than two days a week.

While there is no direct evidence that the indentures of the apprentices ever carried such a clause, there is ample evidence that, up to the end of the eighteenth century, the Thames yielded such a harvest of salmon that it is only reasonable to suppose that people must have got fed up with eating them. It would be a matter for surprise if the apprentices didn't object.

But, by the first quarter of the nineteenth century, Londoners were already beginning to ask where all the salmon had got to. By the 'fifties there was serious alarm over the state of the 'malodorous Thames.' At the time of my story a commission was sitting, ostensibly to find ways of bringing back the salmon; in fact, to preside over an inquest. The river was already dead.

According to Frank Buckland, the Victorian naturalist, the last salmon in the Thames was caught at Windsor in the 1820s by a fisherman named Finmore. The fish made his lie at Surley Hall. When he showed above water the local netsmen planned his destruction. The first attempt to catch him failed because the fish leapt triumphantly over the corks of the seine net. On the second attempt, another net was supported in the air to snare him as he tried to throw himself clear.

When he was grassed, he was offered to George IV, then residing at Virginia Water, who awarded the netter a guinea a pound. The royal bounty was twenty guineas.

But the ichthyologist, William Yarrell, held that Buckland was wrong. Writing in 1836 in his *History of British Fishes* —still regarded as an authoritative work on the subject—he recalled that he had noted the taking of a salmon in the Thames in June, 1833.

But the most valuable information is contained in the minutes of the evidence of the commission which enquired into the state of the salmon fisheries in 1860–1861.

Mr William Flynn declared that on Thursday, October 25th, 1860, he called on Mr Charles of Pimlico, the fishmonger to the Queen, to see the 20-lb. fish alleged to have been caught at Erith in the Thames on October 23rd. He said that it was 'in high condition'—i.e., fresh—but expressed a doubt as to whether the fish had been caught in the Thames at all. He gave no reason for his doubt but, in the modern phrase, implied that he had a hunch. He may have suspected that it came from the Medway.

In Mr Flynn's opinion, the last salmon was taken at Blackwall about 1857. Asked how long it was since salmon were common he replied that, in the year 1816, the Thames had the greatest run ever known. Ninety fish were taken in a single morning. There was such a catch that they fetched only threepence a pound in Billingsgate Market.

The Secretary of the Thames Angling Preservation Society, Mr Henry Farnell, gave evidence. He hadn't seen a fish in the river for thirty-six years although, in his youth, he remembered sixteen fish being caught in a single haul. In his opinion the last salmon was taken in 1829. He added, with significant emphasis, that the Gas Company had become active about 1820.

Mr John Gould, F.R.S., said that there were plenty of salmon in the river about 1820 to 1823; in his opinion the last was killed by a Mr Wilder off Monkey Island in 1830. Mr Richard Lovegrove, of Maidenhead, a son and grandson of Thames fishermen, put the date somewhat earlier—between 1823 and 1824. He was probably referring to that part of the Thames he personally knew. He recalled that, in former years, sixty fish had been taken in a season at Boulter's Lock.

In the course of the enquiry, in which a succession of witnesses confirmed that salmon had been plentiful in the first fifteen years of the century, fascinating facts emerged.

One fisherman stated that the highest point of the river in which salmon had been known to spawn was the Mill at Basildon, near Goring. Another said that the salmon had disappeared because too many exhausted and foul fish had been offered for sale. These kelts were called 'strikes.' Grilse —one-year-at-sea fish—were known as 'harvest cocks.' Samlets of a few inches in length were designated 'skeggars.' Shad, which had been common in the Thames, disappeared at the same time that the salmon disappeared. Asked why Thames fish were esteemed by Londoners, as they were, more than salmon from any other river, another elderly witness wisely retorted that they were better than Scotch salmon because they had not been dead so long.

In the conclusions of the Committee of Enquiry, it was decided that the major causes of the loss of salmon to the Thames were: sewage, discharges from gas works and factories, poisonous drainage from mines, non-observance of close seasons, poaching and unlawful fishing, obstructions caused by weirs and stake nets; and, finally, navigation by steamers.

At this distance of time, it is interesting to analyse what the real causes were. Certainly the coming of the steam-boat wasn't one of them; although the Victorians thought so. In fact, the propellers and the paddles probably helped to oxygenate the fouled water.

All the witnesses at the Commission of Enquiry were agreed that the Thames salmon diminished between 1810 and 1820; disappearing altogether somewhere between the 'twenties and the 'sixties.

The U-bend water-closet was invented in 1810. Until that time most sewage was emptied into cesspools or pits. The solids rotted away and liquids were filtered through the soil before they reached the river. With the introduction of the U-bend, the sewage was flushed straight into the Thames. During the same period, the population of London rose from under a million to nearly three millions in 1861.

In 1858, Mr Disraeli introduced a Bill to levy a special rate on the Metropolis for the purpose of purifying the river and completing the main drainage system, which it was hoped would make the lower reaches of the Thames fit to live beside again. The estimated cost was three million and the outlay was five.

Between 1858 and 1865, the great engineer, Sir Joseph Bazalgette, constructed the system to carry London's sewage to the outfalls at Barking and Crossness. The population was then about three million. Bazalgette reckoned on an increase to about three and a half million. It is a tribute to his genius that the sewage system he built is essentially the same system coping with a population of ten million today.

When the new outfall works were completed, and opened under royal patronage, it was believed that the waters of the Thames would be pure again. In fact, the situation mysteriously deteriorated. Only within recent years has it been discovered that the sewage effluent emptied into the river at the outfalls isn't carried straight down to the sea by the current. Pouring into the river twenty-four hours a day it rocks on the tide and pollutes the water up to the terrace of Parliament itself; that terrace from which some ass of a politician mouthed the sentiment that 'The Thames is liquid history.'

In the Middle Ages, Henry III kept a polar bear in the

Tower, given to him by the King of Norway, which he used to turn out in the river to catch fish for its meals. In the reign of Edward III the Thames fishermen presented a petition to the Crown to prevent farmers in the upper reaches reducing the stock of salmon by shovelling fry for pig food. In 1758, a member of the City Corporation, a Mr Binnell, could write that the Thames abounds with salmon, large flounders, plaice, mullet, whiting, smelts, eels, perch, trout, carp, tench, bream, chub, roach, dace, and gudgeons, besides oysters 'of which these are the finest in the world.'

As late as 1838 the minutes of the celebrated London angling club, the Piscatorial Society, announced a prize for the best salmon taken in the Thames. At that time the fish was a recent memory and still a pious hope. It seems definite that, up to the 'sixties, people believed that the salmon would come back. It is indicative of the obstinacy of the fish that, in the 1930s, five salmon were actually taken out of the Kent tributary of the Thames, the Medway.

In a hopeless endeavour to reintroduce the fish, Buckland and the Thames Preservation Society introduced fry at Hampton Court and other places. Between 1901 and 1909, more sowings of fry were made and Lord Desborough introduced Huchen salmon from the Danube at Taplow. None survived.

No fish could survive in the polluted water between Teddington Lock and Gravesend. As the population of London increased, more clean water was taken from the upper reaches for drinking and other purposes and, as a consequence, more was returned as sewage to the lower part of the river. The claims of the power stations, which take out cold water and return it at such a temperature that the cleansing organisms can't get to work in it, aggravated the problem.

The situation today is that the lower reaches of the Thames are so poisoned that even a shrimp—an animal which I am told needs less oxygen than almost any living creature—can't survive above Gravesend. The water is so full of detergents that the paddles of the ferry-boats, which still ply across the river, stir it up until it foams like a wash-tub. In the summer the surface bubbles with the explosion of methane gas rising from the sludge. In hot weather, the brass on the ships coming into the Pool of London, and the brass of the officers' buttons, goes black in an hour or two. The poison in the water eats holes in the propellers of the river boats. Even chromium plate turns blue.

On those occasions, beloved of gossip writers, when young men coming out of the Savoy show off to their girl friends by jumping into the river in evening-dress to swim to the other side, the wonder isn't that they get across but that they get away with it without being infected with disease. It's probable that the children who still sport about under Tower Bridge have developed antibodies; but, theoretically, anybody who puts his hand in the lower reaches of the river is taking a risk. The Medical Officers of Health simply can't understand why there are not more cases of leptospirosis, or worse. Nevertheless, it is only fair to state that Londoners, in spite of the 'liquid history' on their doorstep, remain surprisingly healthy. But not London's river.

Rose Cottage, Aldworth, Berks
New Year's Eve 1959–1960

ACKNOWLEDGEMENTS

A BOOK of this character can only be written with the help of others. I am especially indebted to Dr M. T. Morgan, C.M.G., M.C., M.D., lately Chief Medical Officer of the Port of London; to Mr A. R. J. Vickery of the Chief Engineer's Department of the London County Council, who guided me on an exhausting tour of the sewers; to Councillor Patrick Murray of Edinburgh, that remarkable bibliophile who can dig up more off-beat information than anybody else I know; to the late Countess Mountbatten of Burma, C.I., G.B.E., D.C.V.O., LL.D.; the past owner of Broadlands, to Dr Victor Goldman, F.F.A.R.C.S., to whom I have never put a question to which, in his generosity and knowledge, he hasn't given me a correct answer; to the Director of the Liverpool Observatory and Tidal Institute; to the Chief Inspector of the Kent River Board for much valuable information about the occurrence of salmon in the Medway; to the librarians of the Thames Conservancy Library, the Guildhall Library, the Royal College of Physicians, the Royal College of Nursing, the London Library, and the archivists of the British Transport Commission. Also to my secretaries, Fay Crowder and Mrs Frederic Lewis in particular, who have helped me in my pregnancy. I ought also to acknowledge my indebtedness to the authors of innumerable period books; but why worry? They won't; they're all as dead as the Thames salmon.